The Maverick

JAN HUDSON

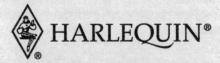

HARLEQUIN®

TORONTO • NEW YORK • LONDON
AMSTERDAM • PARIS • SYDNEY • HAMBURG
STOCKHOLM • ATHENS • TOKYO • MILAN • MADRID
PRAGUE • WARSAW • BUDAPEST • AUCKLAND

Recycling programs
for this product may
not exist in your area.

ISBN-13: 978-0-373-75310-9

THE MAVERICK

Copyright © 2010 by Janece O. Hudson.

ABOUT THE AUTHOR

Jan Hudson, a former college psychology teacher, is a RITA® Award-winning author of thirty books, a crackerjack hypnotist, a dream expert, a blue-ribbon flower arranger and a fairly decent bridge player. Her most memorable experience was riding a camel to visit the Sphinx and climbing the Great Pyramid in Egypt. A native Texan whose ancestors settled in Nacogdoches when Texas was a republic, she loves to write about the variety of colorful characters who populate the Lone Star State: unique individuals who celebrate life with a "howdy" and "y'all come." Jan and her husband currently reside in Austin, and she loves to hear from readers. E-mail her at JanHudsonBooks@gmail.com.

Books by Jan Hudson

HARLEQUIN AMERICAN ROMANCE
1017—THE SHERIFF*
1021—THE JUDGE*
1025—THE COP*
1135—THE REBEL*
1162—THE TEXAS RANGER*
1290—THE TWIN*

SILHOUETTE DESIRE
1035—IN ROARED FLINT
1071—ONE TICKET TO TEXAS
1229—PLAIN JANE'S TEXAN
1425—WILD ABOUT A TEXAN
1432—HER TEXAN TYCOON

*Texas Outlaws

In loving memory of
Kate Duffy

Chapter One

Amazed at how far she'd come in a few months, Cassidy Outlaw jogged along the path beside Austin's Lady Bird Lake without even breaking a sweat. When she'd first started her exercise regimen, she couldn't make half a block without being winded and dying from the burn in her legs. Now she could actually enjoy these early morning jogs.

Especially with the current view to hold her interest.

She trotted behind a very tight set of male buns attached to a terrific torso with a lovely expanse of shoulders. The shorts were black, the T-shirt gray and the hair short, a damp brown, and probably less curly when it was dry. A white towel was draped around his neck.

She liked his legs, too. Well-muscled thighs and calves. Was his front as good as his back? Some good-looking guys ran this trail—and some real dogs. Which was he?

Suddenly, Tight Buns stopped. Cass, being in midstride, didn't, and she couldn't get her footing quickly enough to keep from tripping over him and going down onto the decomposed granite path.

"Ouch! Dammit! Dammit!" She grabbed her knee.

"Oh, God, I'm sorry," Tight Buns said.

"Idiot! What were you thinking, to stop like—" The words died on her lips when she looked up and saw the klutz was no putz. He was an Adonis.

"Are you hurt?" he asked.

Maybe he was a putz, after all. "I figure if there's blood, I'm hurt for sure."

He grabbed the towel from around his neck and dabbed the blood from the scrape on her knee.

"Is that sanitary?" she asked, glaring at him and trying to keep from being mesmerized by a pair of the bluest eyes she'd ever seen. Real baby blues, so pale they seemed to cut into her like lasers.

"Oh, hell! I didn't even think of germs. Let's get some proper first aid." He flagged down a cab, which was a miracle in itself, since Austin didn't have cabs cruising the streets like New York.

Before she could sputter more than, "What the hell do you—" he'd scooped her into his arms and slid her into the backseat.

"To the nearest E.R.," he said to the driver.

"You're nuts! I don't need to go to an emergency room for a skinned knee. I just need some peroxide and a Band-Aid."

"Are you sure?"

"Of course I'm sure."

"Make that the nearest drugstore," he told the driver.

The cab drove a couple of blocks and stopped. "Here we are."

Tight Buns pulled out a twenty from a small zippered pocket and handed it to the driver. "Keep the change," he said, flinging open the door. He reached inside and made to pick her up again, but Cass slapped his hands.

"Have you got any more money in your pocket?" she asked.

He felt inside. "Nope. That was it."

"Keep a couple of bucks for yourself," she told the driver, "and give us the change."

The man didn't look too thrilled, but he handed her a ten. She started to hold out for more, but gave it up and got out.

"Why did you do that?" Tight Buns asked.

"Because the only things in my fanny pack are my car keys and pepper spray." She waved the bill. "This is for first aid supplies."

"Good point. Can you walk?"

"Of course I can walk," Cass said. With blood dribbling down her leg, she marched into the drugstore, Blue Eyes close behind.

Inside, he walked her to the pharmacy area and had her sit on the chair near the blood pressure cuff.

"Stay here and I'll gather the supplies."

In a couple of minutes he was back with a basketful of stuff: gauze pads, peroxide, first aid spray and ointment, tissues, and a big box of Band-Aids.

"Isn't that overkill?" she asked.

He glanced down at the basket. "I don't think so. I wasn't sure what we'd need."

"Have you paid for the items yet?"

"Not yet."

"I didn't think so," Cass said. "You've got more than ten dollars worth there, I'm sure."

"I have a credit card."

"Well, why on earth didn't you say so? I wouldn't have arm wrestled the cab driver for change."

He merely looked at her as if he were indulging a child, and squatted in front of her. After he assembled his supplies, he patted his thigh. "Put your foot up here."

She didn't argue for once.

Very gently, he flushed the area with peroxide, mopping up

spillovers with gauze pads and tissues, squirted a line of ointment along the scrape and topped it with a large bandage. "There."

She studied his handiwork. "Good job. Thanks. I'll be running along now—sorry, I don't even know your name."

He grinned, flashing dimples that made him almost pretty. "Griff. Griffin Mitchell."

She stuck out her hand. "Cass. Cassidy Outlaw."

"How about I buy you breakfast?"

"Thanks," Cass said, "but that's not necessary. I need to get home and dress for work."

"What time do you have to be there?"

"Oh, nine-thirty or ten."

He glanced at his watch. "It's only seven-thirty. We'll make it quick. What do you like?"

"There used to be a great little place on the next block that served the best breakfast tacos you've ever tasted, but it's gone now. That monster of a hotel gobbled up most of the neighborhood." She nodded toward the lakefront and the several stories of concrete and glass where several small businesses had once stood.

"I take it you don't approve."

"You take it right," Cass said. "I miss those tacos."

"How about we try the coffee shop at the hotel?" Griff asked. "My treat."

"Like this?" She looked down at her shorts and dirty T-shirt. "Austin is a supercasual town, but I doubt if they'd let us in the door as grungy as we are."

"Let's storm the gates out of spite." Those blue eyes twinkled with mischief. "I understand the coffee is good and the omelets are first class."

Never one to back away from a challenge, Cass said, "You're on. Let's go."

He paid for the items in his basket, and the cashier, a middle-aged woman with a severe underbite, didn't even mention that they'd been opened. In fact, she was so busy gawking at Griff she could barely wield the scanner. "Did anybody ever tell you that you look like Paul Newman?" she asked, drool practically dripping from the corners of her bulldog mouth.

He smiled. "Once or twice."

Cass hadn't been around for Paul Newman's heyday—she was more familiar with his salad dressing than his early movie roles—and she didn't get the connection at first. Then she remembered a couple of classic films she'd seen on cable. *Butch Cassidy and the Sundance Kid,* of course, and another one in which he'd worn some sort of short toga. She couldn't recall the name of the movie, but she remembered those eyes. They were the same mesmerizing color as Griffin Mitchell's. No wonder women went ape over Newman back then.

"Ready?" Griff asked, touching her back. "Shall I get a taxi?"

She chuckled. "I think I can make it a block or two."

They crossed the street, and she favored her knee slightly as they walked.

"Are you in pain?"

"It smarts a little. Nothing serious," she said. "I'll take a Tylenol later."

"Damn," he said, snapping his fingers. "I should have thought of that. If you'll wait here, I'll run back to the drugstore and get some."

"Whoa." Cass grabbed his arm. "Not necessary. You're making too much of this. I have some in my car."

"If you're sure." He seemed ready to sprint through traffic at her signal.

"Very sure."

She felt a little strange going into the upscale hotel, but Griff walked in as if he owned the place. "Want to wash up first?" he asked.

"That would be great."

They parted at the restrooms, and Cass cleaned up as best she could. She'd give twenty dollars for a brush right then, but settled for a finger comb, then rejoined Griff.

The hostess met them at the door of the coffee shop, to turn them away, Cass figured. Instead, she smiled brightly. "Good morning, Mr. Mitchell. Your usual table?"

"Yes, thank you, Helen." He steered Cass to a window table overlooking the lake and the jogging path.

When they were seated, Cass lifted her eyebrows. "Your *usual* table, Mr. Mitchell?"

"I often stay here when I'm in town. I've been here a lot lately." He opened his menu. "Are you a bacon and eggs person or a fruit and yogurt type?"

"If I can't have breakfast tacos, I'm a French toast and sausage lover. You?"

"I like the omelets here."

Coffee and a pitcher of orange juice arrived, along with a waiter to take their order.

Cass sipped her coffee. "Ahh. Caffeine. So you're in Austin on business?"

"I am."

"What business are you in?" she asked.

"I'm a lawyer."

She chuckled and shook her head. "I might have known."

"You don't like lawyers?"

"Some I do, some I don't. I'm a recovering lawyer myself."

He grinned. Why did he have such devilishly adorable dimples? "How does one become a recovering lawyer?"

"One gives it up for a healthier lifestyle." Cass poured herself some juice.

"I see. And what do you do now?"

"I sell chili."

He laughed. "With beans or without?"

"Bite your tongue, Yankee. No self-respecting Texan puts beans in chili."

"Sorry. Where do you sell this chili?"

"In a little café called Chili Witches up near the capitol. It's a family business that my mother and aunt started years before my sister and I were born. What kind of lawyering brings you to town?"

"I'm doing some research for a client."

"What kind of research?"

He cocked an eyebrow and looked amused. "I thought you said you were a lawyer."

"Ahh," she said. "The confidential kind. I assume you're not a trial lawyer then. Not a defense attorney from back East who has come to defend a dastardly criminal?"

"Nope. I'm more into corporate concerns than drug dealing and murder."

"Is there a difference?"

His eyebrow went up again. "You really are down on the profession, aren't you?"

"Sorry," Cass said. "I went too far. How do you like Austin?"

"It's a fantastic little city. I'm thinking of moving here."

This time her eyebrows went up. "Really?"

After their food was served, they ate and chatted about the town and its various attractions. Casual talk, but unspoken inferences seemed much more intimate. She couldn't quite put her finger on the subtle undercurrents she felt, but they were there.

He was a charmer to be sure. Slick, handsome and magnetizing with those fabulous baby blues. Her own lawyer's antennae went up.

She wouldn't trust the bastard as far as she could throw him.

Chapter Two

Cass would have bet a thousand dollars Griff Mitchell would show up at Chili Witches that day. She would have lost. Guess she'd read the signals wrong. Usually she wasn't so far off.

Oh, well, no big loss. He was a nice looking guy and interesting—even if he was a Yankee lawyer. Her track record with Yankee lawyers wasn't good. Her former fiancé was both. They'd worked for the same New York firm, and he'd sworn his undying love for her when he'd presented her with a large emerald-cut diamond and asked her to marry him. First chance he had to make points with the senior partners, he'd thrown her under the bus for a leg up.

What was worse, he didn't see anything wrong with what he'd done.

Cass couldn't see being married to someone ruled by jungle ethics. She quickly soured on New York, the high-powered firm and the eighteen-hour days. She also missed Austin and her twin sister, Sunny. They'd never been so far apart for so long.

At closing time, Cass locked up behind the last of the staff and stashed the cash in the office safe. As was their custom, she made a final round of Chili Witches, with its rough-hewn walls and over forty years of rotating Texas kitsch. Her New York colleagues would laugh if they could see her now in jeans and a red tee instead of a power suit, but she was happy here among people who mattered.

She was startled when she saw the gray-haired man sitting at a corner table with a cup of coffee. He smiled at her as she approached.

"I'm sorry, sir, but I didn't realize anyone was still here. We're closed. You'll have to leave."

He suddenly vanished. *Poof.* Gone. Her heart jumped into overdrive. *Oh, gawd!* Was she going crazy? Maybe her eyes were playing tricks on her. She double-checked the locks, then hurried out of the café and up the back stairs to her apartment on the second floor.

She locked her door, reset the alarm, slapped her hand on her chest and struggled to keep herself from hyperventilating. No way was she admitting to what she'd seen. Correction: make that what she *thought* she saw. No way.

Not only had the incident scared the pants off her, the whole thing was impossible. Totally, utterly, completely impossible. Snatching up her phone, she punched the speed dial for Sunny, but hung up before it rang. Her sister would never let her hear the end of it if Cass admitted to seeing some sort of apparition. There was some perfectly reasonable explanation for what she thought she'd seen. Perhaps a flicker of a passing car or a glint from streetlights had somehow created an odd image. It had been a long day, and she was tired and ripe for her eyes to play tricks.

Forget it.

Certainly there was no reason to be afraid. After all, there was a cop in the apartment only a few feet away from her front door, and a baseball bat under her bed.

Flipping on the TV to catch the last of the news, she pulled off her sneakers, shed her jeans and tried to get her mind on something else. The phone rang.

"Did you just try to call me?" her sister asked.

"I did, but I hung up before you answered."

Sunny laughed. "When did that ever matter? Something going on?"

While it was true that she and Sunny shared a special bond identical twins often had, and she acknowledged their exceptional connectedness, she didn't want to admit to any absurd woo-woo kind of stuff.

"Cass? What's happened?"

"What makes you think anything happened?"

"Don't try to snow me, sis. Give."

"Well, I met a very interesting man today," Cass said.

"Uh-uh. You meet interesting men all the time. You're nervous. I can hear it in your voice."

"Sunny, I… Promise you won't laugh."

"Cross my heart."

"I think I saw him," she whispered.

"Why are you whispering? And who did you see? The interesting man you met?"

"No. The Senator." Cass heard a choking sound over the phone. "Are you laughing?"

"No, I was coughing. Where did you see him?"

"Maybe I *didn't* see him," Cass said, trying to convince herself as much as Sunny. "I've never seen him before, and it was just for a second. You're the one who always claimed you saw and talked to him, even when we were little. I'm sure it was just my imagination. How are Ben and Jay?"

Ben McKee was a Texas Ranger and Sunny's fiancé; Jay was Ben's five-year-old son.

"They're fine. And don't try to change the subject. Describe your glimpse of the Senator. When did it happen?"

Knowing Sunny wouldn't give up until she heard the whole story, Cass told her when and where she'd seen the man. "He had gray hair and wore a dark gray suit with a red-and-blue tie."

"Sounds like the Senator. Why didn't you talk to him?"

"Exactly how does one talk to a ghost?"

GRIFFIN MITCHELL HUNG UP his coat and stripped off his tie. Damned meetings had gone on all day, and he was tired. He stepped onto the balcony of his hotel room and looked out over the lake, at the reflection of streetlights there. He thought of a pair of dark eyes and a sassy mouth on a beautiful woman—and not for the first time that day. He'd meant to drop by Chili Witches, the café she'd mentioned, but he hadn't been able to break away. He'd known who she was, of course. He'd known a great deal about her and her sister, the ex-cop, who ran the family business now that their mother and aunt had retired. But nobody had prepared him for the sheer vibrancy of Cassidy Outlaw in the flesh.

Cass was an extraordinary lady, but then he was fond of tough Texas women. After all, his mother had been one until she moved to Long Island after she married Griff's father. In fact, she still flew the Texas flag on the patio at their house. Occasionally, she used to turn the cook out of the kitchen and make chili or tacos or some other Tex-Mex concoctions. Griff hadn't much liked the food, but he never knew if he didn't care for the spicy fare in general or if his mother was simply a terrible cook.

In any event, he planned to have chili for lunch the following day. Maybe he could even talk Cass into going out with him Friday night or Saturday. He'd have to check the

Austin American-Statesman he'd bought in the lobby, and find something interesting going on in town. What sort of entertainment would suit Cassidy's taste? He couldn't see either one of them enjoying the doings on Sixth Street—the clubs there were more for a younger crowd—but the dossier he had on her didn't cover entertainment preferences. He'd have to wing it.

GRIFF LOOKED FOR CASS on the jogging trail the next morning, but didn't see her. Probably because of her scraped knee. He was sorry about the injury. That part hadn't been scripted. He skipped out on Friday's meetings in time to arrive at Chili Witches by a quarter of twelve. There was already quite a crowd, he noticed, as he stood by the door and surveyed the place.

He spotted Cass talking and laughing with a table of uniformed cops. When she spotted him, she broke away and approached him.

"Hello," she said, smiling. "Welcome to Chili Witches. Have you been here before?"

A bit puzzled by her behavior, he nevertheless played along. "No. This is a new experience for me. How's your knee today?"

She frowned. "My knee? It's fine. Let me find you a seat. Do you have a preference?"

"Surprise me," he said, grinning.

"Sure. Right this way." She led him to a table for two by the window and plucked a menu from between a small black cauldron of crackers and the saltshaker. "We have three grades of chili—mild, which is comfortably spicy, medium for those who like to sweat a little, and 'hotter than hell,' which has about the same kick as a blow torch and is not for the uninitiated. We also have other dishes, as you can see. Our hamburgers and sandwiches are excellent, as well as our chili, and we have a salad bar. May I get you something to drink?"

"Very good," Griff said.

"I beg your pardon?"

"Your spiel. Well done."

She frowned again. "Thank you, I think. Drink?"

"Beer would be good."

"I'll have it out right away." She smiled and left.

The whole exchange seemed very peculiar to Griff. Surely he didn't look so different in his suit that she failed to recognize him. He studied the menu and opted for the house specialty, mild.

A waiter in a red T-shirt and jeans, which seemed to be the uniform, delivered the beer and took his order.

"Where is Cass?" Griff asked.

"I don't know," the waiter said. "She didn't come in today."

"How can that be? I just spoke to her."

The waiter chuckled. "That wasn't Cass. That was Sunny, her twin sister. Happens all the time. Sunny's here Monday, Wednesday and Friday, and Cass takes over on Tuesday, Thursday and Saturday."

"Oh, I see. I knew Cass had a sister, but I didn't realize they were twins."

"Identical. Some people say they can tell them apart, but me, I can't tell one from the other. I'll be right back with your chili. Want cheese or oyster crackers with that?"

"Sure." It was a shame he'd picked the wrong day to visit the café, and was risking heartburn for nothing. At least the beer was cold.

While he waited, Griff looked around at the scarred tables and rough, wooden walls covered with all sorts of garish memorabilia. He doubted that much had changed in the past forty years. The bar looked as if it might be original to the building, which was well over a hundred years old. Unbelievable that this place sat on such a prime piece of real estate. He wondered if Cass and her sister realized the value of the land.

Of course they did. Cass was nobody's fool, and her sister had identical genes.

When his chili was served, he picked up his spoon with trepidation, but his first bite was a pleasant surprise. It must have been his mother's terrible cooking to blame for his previous opinion. A good thing the food was tolerable since he'd have to make a return trip the next day.

CASS'S CELL PHONE RANG just as she was locking the door to her apartment. It was Sunny.

"What's up, sis?"

"Did that new guy you met have unusual blue eyes and a Yankee accent?" Sunny asked.

"Yes, why?"

"I think he's having a bowl of chili at table four. He asked me how my knee was doing. You might want to make a pass through here if you're interested."

"Thanks for the heads-up," Cass told her. "I'm due someplace shortly, but I'll check it out."

Her first impulse was to go back inside and change clothes. Stupid idea. She looked just fine in pants and sandals, and comfort was important for the volunteer work she intended for the afternoon. Griffin Mitchell was no big deal, she told herself. Still, she took the steps a little faster than she usually did.

She spotted Griff at table four, dressed in an expensive suit and chowing down on a bowl of chili. "Well, how is it?" she asked as she approached.

He glanced up and smiled warmly, flashing those cute

dimples again. "Quite good." He glanced toward the door where Sunny stood, then back at her. "Cass?"

"In person."

"Won't you join me?"

"For a moment," she said. "I have to be somewhere in a few minutes."

"Can't you play hooky for the afternoon? You can show me the sights of Austin."

"Sorry, but I've volunteered to stuff envelopes for a non-profit organization, and since I'm the president, it would look bad if I was a no-show."

"I concede your point. Would you like some lunch?"

"I've already eaten, thanks, but I'll have a glass of iced tea and keep you company if you'd like."

His dimples flashed. "I'd like."

Cass signaled a waiter for tea.

"How's your knee today? Your sister said hers was fine and looked at me as if I had grown horns as long as those." He motioned to the rack of a longhorn on the wall.

She chuckled. "Got us mixed up, did you? A common occurrence. My knee is fine, too. I'm a fast healer."

He motioned to his bowl. "This really is very good. You ought to consider packaging and marketing it."

"We're looking into the possibility. Think they would buy it in… You know, I don't think you've mentioned where you're from."

"I grew up on Long Island. And I'm sure at least one person there would buy it. My mother. She's a Texas girl."

"Really? So you're not a total foreigner." Cass checked her watch. Karen would kill her if she didn't get there to help. "Griff, I'm sorry, but I can't stay longer. I have to get to my task." She stood.

He stood as well and peeled a twenty from the wad in his money clip, tossing it on the table. "I'll go with you. You could probably use an extra pair of hands, and I'm not bad at stuffing envelopes."

Chapter Three

"See, I told you it would all come back to me," Griff said as he licked another envelope from his stack. He'd shed his coat and tie rolled up his shirtsleeves and dived in.

"I'm proud of you," Cass said. "How long since you've actually stuffed any mail?"

"In bulk? Must have been in college, or maybe in law school when I was working on some campaign or another."

"Where did you go to law school?"

"Harvard."

"Of course," Cass said. "Why did I even ask?"

"And you?"

"University of Texas, here in Austin. I was too poor for Harvard or Yale, and I got an excellent education here."

"I'm sure you did," Griff said. "UT Law has a fine reputation. Too bad you're not using your education."

Cass's hackles went up. "Oh, but I am. My education doesn't define me. It enriches me."

"Sorry. That was insensitive. You're right, of course."

"Are you being condescending?"

He smiled and held up his hands in surrender. "With a tough Texas woman? I wouldn't dare. I'm done with my stack. Are there more?"

"That's all," Cass said. "Karen will stamp them in the morning when she comes in, and deliver them to the post office."

Griff picked up one of the envelopes and looked at the return address. "Exactly what is POAC?"

"Didn't you read one of the letters?" Cass asked.

"Nope, I simply stuffed and licked."

She chuckled. "You could have spent the last two hours aiding and abetting a subversive organization. Lawyers are supposed to read the fine print."

"I trusted you wouldn't get us thrown in the slammer. Let's see. POAC. Please Order Another Chili. People on a Caper. Pick Out a Cucumber."

Cass laughed. "How about Preserve Old Austin's Charm? We pronounce the acronym 'poe-ack.' We're sort of a watchdog group to help preserve the flavor of our town so that its charm doesn't get paved over by cookie cutter high-rises and such."

"Ah, like the taco place and the hotel."

"Exactly. We're not extremists opposed to progress and modernization, but we want to keep the old along with the new. Austin has made a half-dozen lists recently as one of the best places in the country to live, and we've had a big influx of people. Sometimes it seems as if, after they arrive, they want to start changing the very things that drew them here, to make Austin into Anywhere, USA."

"You sound very passionate about this," Griff said.

"I am. I love this town. I love the bakeries and shoe shops and little taco joints that have been downtown for fifty or a hundred years."

"And the chili cafés?"

Cass gave a bark of laughter. "You bet. But Chili Witches wasn't always a café. It started out as a saloon and bawdy house."

He chuckled. "You're kidding."

"I kid you not. The madam's name was Selma Newton, and she was a real rounder. Upstairs, where my apartment is, used to be rooms where the soiled doves entertained the town swells."

"You live over the restaurant?"

"Temporarily. Until I can get this place fixed up," she said.

"Which place? Here?" he asked, looking around the living room of the run-down house where they'd come to work.

"Yes. When I'm finished it will be a charming cottage again, and in a prime location. The architecture is unique, and while they may not qualify as landmarks when this block is restored all the houses will be lovely. Can you believe they wanted to tear down these houses and put up another five-story apartment building? And you should have seen the design!"

"Bad, huh?"

"Atrocious!" Cass said, making a face.

"And POAC stopped it?"

"Not single-handedly. Several groups and individuals joined together, lobbied for the preservation of the neighborhood and bought the properties."

"And you bought this house?"

"I did. And the one next door, as well."

Griff lifted his eyebrows. "So don't mess with Texas women?"

Cass grinned. "You got it, Yankee. Now I'll get off my soapbox. Thanks for helping me this afternoon. May I drop you at your hotel?"

"I was hoping you might show me around some of charming Austin this afternoon," Griff said as she locked up.

She glanced at her watch. "I have time for a drive through Zilker Park, but I have an appointment coming up."

"I noticed that there was an interesting production at the

Paramount Theater this weekend. Would you like to go with me tomorrow night?"

"I'd love to go, but I work on Saturdays," Cass said. "We don't close until ten or ten-thirty. Sorry."

"I know it's short notice, but could you make it tonight if I can get tickets?"

"Good luck with that," Cass said. "I hear it's sold out."

He grinned. "Never underestimate my ability to get what I want."

She threw back her head and laughed. "I wouldn't dare."

GRIFF HAD TO CALL IN a couple of favors, and ended up paying a scalper an exorbitant price, but he got two tickets in the orchestra, fifth row center, for that night's performance at the theater on Congress Street. He'd have paid twice the amount. Not only was it a sop to his ego, but he wanted to impress Cass. He found that he genuinely liked her and enjoyed her company. She was the most interesting and engaging woman he'd met in a very long time.

As soon as the tickets were assured, he called the cell phone number she'd given him and told her the show was a go.

"Wonderful!" she said. "Now I have someplace to show off my new pedicure. My toes are absolutely ravishing."

He laughed. "Your appointment was for a pedicure?"

"Along with a haircut. Do you think it was fate?"

"Undoubtedly. The performance starts at eight. Shall we have dinner beforehand or a late supper?"

"I'm not a late supper kind of gal," Cass said, "and I'm going to be pushed to get home and dress. Why don't you order something nice from room service, and I'll have a bite at home? We can have drinks at the theater. Shall I pick you up?"

"No, I have a car at my disposal. I'll pick *you* up. Seven?"

"Seven is great. Just come up the stairs off the parking lot behind the café. I'm apartment B. And Griff, remember that Austin is supercasual. People will be in everything from shorts and flip-flops to dress clothes. Feel free to go without a tie."

"My mother would disown me. She was from Dallas."

"Ahh," Cass said. "Enough said. Dallas has always been much more fashion conscious than Austin."

When he picked up Cass later, he would have debated Austinites' fashion sense. She looked stunning in a blue dress and a floaty, flowered jacket. The high heeled sandals she wore were little more than thin straps to show off her newly painted pink toenails, but he'd been around women enough to know that she hadn't gotten them at Wal-Mart.

"You look lovely," he told her. "I like your toes."

She laughed and wiggled them. "Terribly Pink."

"Yes, they are."

"The color is Terribly Pink."

"Ahh. Excuse my faux pas."

Downstairs, he helped her into the backseat of the chauffeured Town Car he'd hired for the evening.

"How very impressive," Cass said when they were settled.

"That was the idea," he said, winking. "This smells much better than most taxis. And it's more comfortable. I was hoping you would appreciate it."

"I do. I do." To the driver she said, "Hi, Brad. How are you? I haven't seen you in ages."

"I'm fine, thank you," he responded as he pulled away.

"How's Barbara?" she asked.

"Great. She's pregnant."

"How wonderful! This is your first, isn't it?"

"Yes, it is. We're excited."

"You know our driver?" Griff asked.

"Sure. Brad's wife, Barbara, used to work at Chili Witches when they were in college and before they started their car and limo service. Austin has grown over the years, but basically we're still like a small town."

"You've convinced me."

"Actually, the theater's not far from here," Cass said. "Walking distance if I'd worn more sensible shoes."

"I'm glad you didn't. I rather like those. Jimmy Choo?"

"Prada," she said. "How on earth do you know about Jimmy Choo?"

"You caught me." He laughed. "I confess I watched a couple of episodes of *Sex and the City* to see what all the fuss was about. I discovered it wasn't a guy thing, but I do recall Jimmy Choo as being a coveted kind of shoe. I seem to remember Prada as being in the same category."

A few minutes later they were standing in front of the old theater on Congress, the wide street that led from the front of the capitol building to the river, then many miles to the south beyond that. The Paramount was, according to Cass, over a hundred years old and looked rather ordinary from the outside. Inside was another story.

"I can't believe this place," Griff said. "It looks like a European opera house."

"Beautiful, isn't it? Sunny and I used to beg to come here all the time when we were little. It seemed very grand to us."

"It *is* very grand. And only a little frayed around the edges."

"There was a move to have the place razed a few years ago. Wouldn't that have been a shame?" Cass said.

"I'll have to admit that it would have."

They stopped to have a glass of wine before the show, and after they were served, Griff said, "You've mentioned that your sister's name is Sunny. Is that a nickname?"

"Yes. Her real name is Sundance, but no one has ever called her that."

"What an odd name. Sundance…and Cassidy? Don't tell me—"

Cass chuckled. "I'm afraid so. Our father was named Butch Cassidy Outlaw. His father seemed to think naming his sons after infamous outlaws was a tremendous PR ploy for business or politics or professions in the law. He was Judge John Wesley Hardin Outlaw. Our uncle was a junior, called Wes, and our father was half of the infamous pair played by Paul Newman and Robert Redford in the movie. My uncle Wes became a sheriff, and my father became a state senator, so I suppose my grandfather's idea worked.

"I have several cousins also named after outlaws, and most of them went into law enforcement of one sort or another, and so a tradition was born."

"And you became a lawyer," Griff said.

"I did. And my sister became a cop."

"Were you influenced by family tradition?"

"Hmm. I don't think so. It just seemed to work out that way. Why did you become a lawyer?" Cass asked.

"Tradition again, I suppose. My father and grandfather were lawyers."

"Interesting, isn't it? That we are—were—both third-generation lawyers."

He raised his glass. "To tradition."

"To tradition," she echoed, touching her glass to his.

Suddenly, both glasses shattered. Crystal shards and wine flew everywhere.

Chapter Four

"What the—" Griff spun around to see what had happened. A pair of rowdy boys had smashed into them, knocking their glasses together and breaking them.

The taller of the two looked sheepish and mumbled an apology.

Griff turned back to Cass. "Are you all right?"

"Just a little wet, I think. I feel a little like a ship being launched." She dabbed at her jacket with a napkin.

"My God! You have blood on your cheek."

She reached toward her face.

"Wait. Don't touch it. You may have glass in the cut."

"It can't be too bad. It doesn't hurt."

"I think it should be looked at by a doctor," Griff said.

"Maybe I can help," a woman standing near them offered. "I'm a dermatologist. Come over to where the light's better."

They moved out of the crowd and the doctor looked at Cass's cheek carefully.

"What do you think?" Griff asked.

"I think she's very lucky that she didn't get that nick in her eye. No major harm done. A dab of antiseptic ointment ought to do. Now the dress, I don't know. Isn't that silk?"

Cass chuckled. "It is."

"If I were you, I wouldn't let the stain set," the doctor said. She rummaged in her purse. "Ah, here's a sample that will do the trick." She handed Cass a small tube of ointment.

"Thanks," Cass said, handing her a Chili Witches card. "Drop by for a complimentary bowl of chili. Tell your waiter Cass sent you."

"Thanks, I'll do that. I've been there before, and I love your chili. Are you the manager?"

"My sister and I run it for the family."

"Great to meet you. I'm Bev Strong, by the way."

The dermatologist returned to her party, and Griff said, "I think I should call the car and get you home."

"No way. I'm dying to see this show. My cheek will be fine." Cass held up the tube. "And the dress is only a dress. I'll run to the ladies' room and tend to the damage. Be right back."

Griff watched her walk away, marveling at not only the sexy swing of her hips but also the fact that she hadn't let the accident ruin the evening. Again he thought how different she was from most of the women he dated.

Every time he was around Cass, he found her more and more intriguing. And more and more tempting. Too often he found himself thinking about her lips and her long legs, and weaving fantasies about both. Instead of charming her as he'd intended, he was discovering that she was the one wielding the flute.

He would have to watch that. Getting seriously involved with one of the principals wasn't part of the plan.

Cass returned in a short time, and they took their places for the performance. The seats were excellent, as was the show.

When they were leaving the theater, Griff asked, "Want to stop somewhere for a drink and a bite to eat?"

"Sure," Cass said. "There's a great place just a few blocks from here that you might like. They have a fantastic wine selection and serve Spanish style tapas."

Brad was waiting with the car, and he drove them the few blocks to the spot she'd suggested. Other theatergoers seemed to have the same idea, so the place was filling up, but they found a vacant table in a back corner.

"I adore tapas," Cass said. "I even like to order from the appetizer menu at regular restaurants so I can have a little bit of everything." She picked up her menu and scanned all the interesting selections. "What are your favorites?"

"Since you're familiar with the house specialties," Griff said, "you choose the food, and I'll pick the wine."

"Fair enough, but you might be sorry. I wasn't kidding when I said I like to try some of everything. I'll limit myself to four dishes. We must have the goat cheese cakes with lavender honey, and the spinach empanadas. Do you like scallops?"

"I like everything except liver and grasshoppers."

Cass smiled. "You're safe then. I hate liver, too, and I don't see grasshoppers on the menu. We can have the sea scallops wrapped in basil leaves and ham, and either the crawfish cakes or the roasted piquillo peppers."

"Aren't crawfish sort of like grasshoppers?"

"Bite your tongue, Yankee. Crawfish are more like shrimp. We'll have the crawfish cakes. Trust me, they're delicious here. Or maybe you'd rather have some fruit and cheese."

"Get both."

"Don't tempt me," Cass said. "I warned you that I like some of everything."

"Then order some of everything."

She chuckled. "I'll restrain myself. I doubt if we can make a dent in the ones I mentioned."

"Then we'll take a doggy bag."

"Doggy bag, my foot. We'll take a Cass container. I don't have a dog. I don't even have a cat, though I've been thinking of getting one. Sunny is always after me to adopt one, and I kind of like cats."

A waiter came and took their order. Griff chose a wine Cass had never heard of, but she had no doubt it would be excellent. He was that kind of guy. And, as it turned out, the wine was superb.

"Do you have a pet?" Cass asked him.

"Lord, no. I don't even have a live plant in my apartment. I'm gone so much that it's impractical. If I settle in Austin, I might get a dog. I've wanted one since I was a kid, but my younger brother had allergies, so I had to be content with fish. It's not the same."

"Kind of hard to play fetch with a fish."

He laughed. "True."

"What kind of dog do you want?"

"I'm not sure."

"You need to talk to Sunny or to Skye, my cousin's wife. Sunny volunteers at one of the animal shelters, and she's always looking for good homes for the cats and dogs there. Skye's a veterinarian and a bit fey. She could probably look at you and recommend the perfect pet."

"That sounds interesting."

"She's an interesting lady. All my relatives are interesting. In fact, I'll be seeing several of them on Sunday. We're having a bluebonnet picnic. Maybe you'd like to come along. I'm sure you'd be welcome."

He grinned. "You're eating bluebonnets?"

"Not that I know of. It's sort of an anniversary party and celebration of the bluebonnets for a couple of my first cousins.

They had a double wedding in a bluebonnet field before Sunny and I met them last year."

Griff frowned. "You just met your cousins last year?"

"It's a long and complex story. Ah, here's our food. I'm famished."

The table was so filled with the variety of delicacies she'd ordered that Cass had a difficult time knowing where to start. She reached for a small spinach empanada and took a bite. "Ah, heavenly. Here, taste." She held out the other half, and he ate it from her hand.

"Very good. Are you going to feed me the rest of the meal?"

Smiling, Cass said. "Nope. Grab your fork. It's every man for himself."

They tasted everything, then chose their favorites. The wine was an ideal complement.

"Tell me about your long-lost cousins," Griff said as he helped himself to another scallop.

"Well, they weren't exactly lost. Sunny and I knew about them, but they didn't know about us. We were, as they used to say, born on the wrong side of the blanket." When Griff looked puzzled, she said, "We were illegitimate. Our father was married to someone else when we were conceived, and he died before we were born. To give him credit, he loved my mother deeply, but his wife wouldn't consent to a divorce. Someone shot him on the steps of the capitol before he could convince her to let him go."

"Shot him? Who?"

Cass shrugged. "Nobody knows. His murder was never solved. Anyhow, my mother thought the Outlaw family would consider us an embarrassment, so we never met any of them, and none of the Outlaws knew about us until Sam Bass Outlaw, one of my cousins who's a Texas Ranger, came into

Chili Witches a few months ago. Since then, we've become great friends. Seems that none of them cared much for Iris, the Senator's wife, and she remarried and moved to Ohio or Iowa or somewhere years ago."

"Fascinating."

"Isn't it? Sounds like a soap opera or something. There was never any secret about who our father was, but Mom conveniently neglected to mention that they weren't married. We stumbled on that bit of information ourselves. Mom is going to be mortified to know we've met all our Outlaw relatives and love them."

"She doesn't know you've met them?"

"Nope. And she and Aunt Min will be arriving from France in a few weeks, and the you-know-what's going to hit the fan. Are you going to eat that last crawfish cake?"

"Want to flip for it?"

She laughed. "See, I told you crawfish was good."

"I bow to your good judgment."

They ordered more crawfish cakes and another bottle of wine, and talked about everything in the world. When the waiter began to hover and Cass noticed that the bar was almost empty, she glanced at her watch.

"Dear Lord! Look at the time! It's two in the morning, and I have to work tomorrow."

"Two? I can't believe it." Griff motioned for the check and handed the waiter his credit card. "Sorry I've been so thoughtless. Let's get you home and into bed."

Cass lifted her brows at him, and he gave her an innocent look. "No double entendre intended." Then he spoiled his comment with a wolfish grin.

She laughed and gathered her purse. Griff was the most fascinating man she'd met in ages, and she could go swimming in those eyes of his. Was the giddiness she felt from the wine or his charm? *Remember he's a New York lawyer,* she reminded herself, *and he studied Charm 101 at Harvard.*

Still, despite her own admonitions, a shiver went up her spine when he touched his hand to her back as they left. The man was another heartbreaker, but her hormones didn't seem to care. If she was smart, she'd drop him like a hot rock. Now.

But instead of thinking of ways to discourage him, all her mind could conjure up were visions of silk sheets and a hot mouth.

ON THE DRIVE BACK to her apartment, Griff had to clutch his thighs to keep from taking Cass in his arms and kissing her. He'd never wanted to kiss a woman so badly. He hesitated, not wanting to rush her, nor embarrass her with the driver present. Griff wanted to do more than kiss her, but he blocked those thoughts as best he could.

Should he accept her invitation to the picnic Sunday? *Yes,* he decided. Ingratiating himself with her family couldn't hurt.

"Were you serious about my going with you to the picnic on Sunday?" he asked as they walked upstairs to her apartment.

She hesitated for a millisecond, and his heart lost a beat. He prayed she wasn't having second thoughts about him.

"Of course. I can pick you up at your hotel about ten-thirty, and we'll drive to Wimberley."

"Wimberley?"

"My cousin Belle and her husband live there. It's a small village southwest of here, very picturesque. It's casual. Jeans or shorts."

When they reached her door, she turned and lifted her face. Kissing her was the most natural thing in the world.

And the most mind-blowing. He had the strangest urge to

throw her over his shoulder, beat his chest and carry her into his cave. She would have hated it.

Ignoring the urges he felt, he smiled and said, "I'll see you on Sunday."

ABOUT MIDAFTERNOON ON Saturday, a florist box arrived for Cass. She took it to her office to avoid the curiosity of her staff. Inside she found three perfect yellow roses and an adorable stuffed kitten with big round eyes and a stitched smile.

The card read: "Thank you for a wonderful evening. Maybe this kitty will do until you can have a real one. I'll be the one pacing eagerly in front of my hotel on Sunday morning. Griff."

She put the roses in a bud vase from the supply closet and hugged the kitten. How dear of him to remember her comments about a cat.

She smiled. Charm 101 again. She had his number for sure, but it was fun playing the game. And it was only a game, a flirtation. Despite his interest in moving to Austin, she suspected he'd be gone in a week or two.

Chapter Five

Griff was true to his word. When Cass pulled up to the front of his hotel at ten-thirty on Sunday morning, he was waiting by the door. He wore khaki shorts, some high-end sport shoes and a pale blue polo shirt the exact color of his eyes. He looked good enough to eat with pecans and fudge sauce.

He broke into a grin when he saw her drive up in her little red convertible. "Good morning," he said, climbing in. "I love a woman who is punctual."

"That's me."

She'd worn khaki shorts as well, but her shirt was red and her shoes were a third the cost of his. But then, she told herself, she wasn't interested in engaging in a fashion price war. Today was for fun and comfort. When he was buckled up, she headed through town toward Mo-Pac, the freeway that ran along the railroad track and would take them southwest to join up with the more scenic route to Wimberley.

"I like your ponytail," he said. "It makes you look like a teenager."

"I wish," Cass said. "I love to ride with the top down on days like today, and a ponytail is the easiest way to cope with the blowing hair problem. Isn't the weather gorgeous? March and April are the very best times of the year in Texas. The wildflowers are blooming and the temperature is pleasant. By May many days will hit ninety degrees, and by August it's hotter than Hades. I guess it's a trade-off for not having to deal with snowplows."

"It doesn't snow in Austin?"

"Occasionally. I think we got about an inch in a brief snowfall four or five years ago. And sometimes we get ice, but it's usually gone in a day or so and everybody is running around in flip-flops again."

"Tell me about where we're going," Griff said.

"Well, first we're going to Wimberley to the Burrells' house. That's Gabe and my cousin Belle Starr Outlaw Burrell. We're meeting my sister and her fiancé Ben as well as my cousin Sam Bass Outlaw and his wife, Skye."

"She's the veterinarian."

"Right. And she's also Gabe's sister. I think one of the Naconiche cousins and his wife will be there, or maybe two of them."

"Two of who?"

"Two of the cousins. Three of the Outlaw brothers live in Naconiche, but they don't usually come all at one time. There's J.J., the sheriff, whose name is Jesse James Outlaw, Judge Frank James Outlaw and the homicide cop turned professor, Cole Younger Outlaw. And assorted wives and children will be there, depending on who shows up."

"I hope I can get them all sorted out."

Cass laughed as she hit the open road and floored it. The scarf that had been holding her ponytail went flying behind them, but she didn't stop for it. "Sometimes *I* can't keep them all straight. Hold the wheel for a minute."

"What the—" Griff grabbed the steering wheel while she caught her whipping hair in a rubber band.

"Thanks."

"Do you get many tickets?" he asked.

"For what?"

"Speeding, reckless driving, that sort of thing."

She laughed. "Never. Don't tell me you're one of those nervous nellies." No sooner were the words out her mouth than she saw red-and-blue flashing lights behind her.

Griff merely lifted his eyebrows.

Cursing her big mouth and her heavy foot, Cass pulled over. When she looked in her rearview mirror and got a glimpse of the state trooper exiting his car, she bit back a grin. When he walked up to her window, the grin broke loose. "Hey, Paul. Long time, no see."

His eyes widened, then his grin matched hers. "Cass? Sunny?"

"The former. How are you doing these days?"

"I'm doing fine, Cass. I see you're still driving like a bat out of hell."

She shrugged. "I'm just so glad to be back in Texas, my old habits got the best of me. How are your mama and daddy?"

"They're doing fine. Daddy says he's going to retire next year." The trooper glanced over at Griff and touched the brim of his cowboy hat.

"Paul, this is Griff Mitchell. Griff, Paul used to live down the street from us when we were growing up. Sunny and I used to babysit him."

Griff only nodded.

"We're on our way to Wimberley to celebrate my cousins' anniversary," Cass told Paul. "One of them is a Texas Ranger. You may know him. Sam Outlaw."

"Hell, yes, I know Sam. I didn't know he was married. And I didn't know he was your cousin."

She nodded. "He is. And Sunny's engaged to another Ranger. Ben McKee."

"You don't say. Don't believe I've met him. Tell her hello for me. Listen, Cass, I'm going to give you a pass this time, but I'm going to follow along on your tail for a bit to keep you honest."

She gave him her most dazzling smile. "Thanks, Paul. I appreciate it."

When she pulled away, Griff said, "Do you know everybody in this part of Texas?"

Cass laughed. "Seems that way sometimes. You have to remember the Austin I grew up in was more small town than big city. And folks I didn't know from school or the neighborhood I knew from Chili Witches. Everybody in town ate there or worked there at one time or another."

She watched her speed until she reached Dripping Springs and turned left toward Wimberley. Paul waved and continued straight on Highway 290. She honked and returned his wave.

"Are you going to start speeding again now?" Griff asked.

"I've always been a maverick," she said with a devilish smile.

GRIFF SAT BACK AND enjoyed the ride and the view—of both the countryside and the driver. Cass Outlaw was indeed a maverick. Not only was she extremely attractive, she also had a sharp mind, a charming wit and an unpretentious warmth. She was like no woman he'd ever met, and she intrigued the hell out of him.

He couldn't imagine any young lawyer tossing a fast track career with such a prestigious law firm in New York and returning to Texas to serve chili. It didn't compute. The firm had been very pleased with her work—he'd talked with one of the partners at Baylor Croft & Wiggins—and they had offered her incentives to stay. He wondered if there had been another reason for her leaving besides simply wanting to get back to Austin. What had caused her to now hotly disdain her chosen profession?

"A dollar for your thoughts," Cass said.

"I was wondering how you could have avoided a speeding ticket all these years."

She laughed but didn't ease off the accelerator. "I fibbed a tiny bit. But I haven't had many. In Texas we can take a defensive driving course, and any moving traffic violation won't go on your record."

"How many times have you taken the course?"

"A few." She slowed a bit. "Wimberley is just ahead. It's a charming little town with lots of artistic types. In fact Gabe and Skye's mother is a painter and owns a gallery downtown. Skye's father was a well-known potter."

"Gabe and Skye had different fathers?"

"Yes. Gabe's father was originally from Wimberley, and he inherited property from his grandparents. As I recall, his father died in an accident when he was very young and his mother, Flora, married Skye's father, the potter, and they moved to Wimberley. It took me a while to get it all sorted out as well."

"What does Gabe do?" Griff asked.

"I believe he's in real estate and insurance," she said. She turned off the highway and, after a bit, turned in to a gated area with a guard.

"Hi, Pete. We're expected."

"Yes, ma'am." The big man smiled and touched the brim of his ball cap. "Your sister and her party came through a little while ago. Just drive on up to the helicopter pad, and Gabe will be back to pick you up in a little bit."

"Thanks, Pete." Cass roared off along a winding road.

"We're going by helicopter?" Griff asked.

"Looks like it."

They drove past a pasture with horses, a large house and various outbuildings, until they reached an area where several cars were parked. Obviously, Gabe Burrell was quite successful. Cass's sister, Sunny, sat on the fender of an SUV. A man nearby was giving a small boy a boost up a tree. All three waved as they pulled up and parked.

"We're going to ride in a helicopter!" the boy shouted, pointing to the pad.

"I know," Cass said. "Won't that be fun?" She introduced Griff to Sam McKee, Sunny's fiancé, and Jay, his son.

"Jimmy and Janey are already here," Jay said. "And another one of their cousins. The little kids didn't come."

"Who did come?" Cass asked Sunny.

"As I understand," she said, "Frank and Carrie stayed in Naconiche to babysit the younger children so that everybody else could make it."

"Look," Jay shouted, pointing at the sky.

A sleek blue chopper hovered over their area, then set down on the pad. The boy jumped up and down with excitement, and his father could hardly restrain him until the door opened.

The pilot, a smiling blond man about Griff's age, motioned them aboard. Everybody ducked under the blades and loaded onto the craft. Griff brought up the rear, admiring Cass's lovely long legs and shapely butt as she climbed in ahead of him.

"Gabe Burrell," the pilot shouted, offering Griff his hand. "Welcome to the celebration."

"Thanks. Griff Mitchell. Sweet machine you have."

"Just traded up for it. She's a honey. Fasten your seat belts, and let's go see the bluebonnets."

When everyone was secure, Gabe lifted off and swung

south over rolling hills dotted here and there with color. *Nice view,* Griff thought, *but hardly spectacular.* A few minutes later, he had to retract that when they topped a rise and a valley of blue seemed to stretch for miles.

"Wow!" he said.

"Indeed," Cass said, speaking loudly over the roar of the engine. "Gabe helped Mother Nature along. He scattered thousands of seeds here to make sure we had a good showing this year."

They made two circles, then set down in a field of blue flowers a short distance away from a canopy set up by a winding stream. Several people were standing outside waving.

"Talk about a photo op," Griff said. "And I didn't bring my camera."

"I did," Cass told him. "I'll share pictures." She pulled a camera from her bag and began snapping the moment she stepped off the helicopter. Then she grabbed his hand, "Come on, and I'll introduce you to everybody. Uncle Wes! Aunt Nonie!" she yelled, waving. "Hi, everybody!"

Trotting along behind her, Griff met the gray-haired couple who were the former sheriff of Naconiche and his wife, a retired schoolteacher who now ran an ice cream parlor on the town square.

"Griff, this is J.J. and Mary Beth. J.J. is the sheriff of Naconiche and Mary Beth owns the Twilight Inn and Tearoom."

Griff shook hands with the tall, dark-haired J.J. and nodded to his pretty blonde wife. They exchanged a few words. Soon another couple joined them—Cole, who was even taller than J.J., and a former cop who had turned to college teaching, and his wife Kelly Martin-Outlaw.

"Kelly's a doctor," Cass told Griff. "Actually, we have several doctors in the family, but she's a medical doctor. Cole is a Ph.D. and teaches criminal justice, and Skye is a vet. Where is Skye?"

"She and Sam are driving over from San Antonio," Cole said. "They should be here any minute."

"Speak of the devil," J.J. said, pointing toward a vehicle coming down the lane. "Here they are. Griff, you want a beer?"

"Sure."

"Cooler's this way. Come on, Cole, let's get this guy a beer." J.J. slapped an arm around Griff's shoulders and steered him toward the canopy.

Along the way, a tall dark-haired woman stopped them. "Hello," she said, smiling and offering her hand. "You must be Griff. I'm Belle Outlaw Burrell, sister to these brutes. Welcome to my bluebonnet farm."

"This is your place?" Griff asked.

"Sure is. Gabe's wedding present to me. Isn't it beautiful? We were married here, along with Sam and Skye."

"Happy anniversary," Griff said.

"Thanks, I—"

"We don't have time to chitchat now, sis," J.J. said. "We're headed for the beer before Sam gets to it and drinks it all up."

Belle laughed. "I don't think you have to worry. We have enough for a large army. Where's Flora?"

"I haven't seen her," Cole said. "Did she come with you?" he asked Griff.

"Who's Flora?" Griff asked, trying to keep everybody straight.

"Gabe and Skye's mother."

He shook his head. "She wasn't in our group."

"She's not terribly fond of flying," Belle said. "I think she and Suki must be driving out from the ranch with the rest of the food."

"Belle," J.J. said. "Beer."

"Don't let me stop you." She made a sweep of her hand toward the coolers.

Cole plunged a big hand into the ice and pulled out three cans, popped the tops and handed them out.

"Save some for me," a man yelled, coming toward them.

J.J. retrieved another beer and tossed it toward the approaching man, who was dressed, like the others, in jeans and a T-shirt.

He was obviously an Outlaw brother. They all looked remarkably similar. Tall, dark-haired and handsome. And tough looking. Cole, the professor, was the toughest looking of the lot.

"Griff," J.J. said, "this tall drink of water is our baby brother, Sam. He's the Lone Ranger."

"Texas Ranger to you, snot-face." He stuck out his hand and grinned. "Good to meet you, Griff. That's my wife, Skye, talking to Sunny and Cass."

"Griff," the professor said, "what line are you in?"

"I'm a lawyer."

"From New York?"

"That's right. But my mother was born in Dallas."

J.J. grinned. "Well, looky there. You got some good blood going for you."

"What kind of law do you practice?" Cole asked.

Feeling strongly like a teenager being grilled by his prom date's father, Griff took a swig of his beer. "Corporate."

"Did you and Cass know each other in New York?" J.J. asked.

"No, we met in Austin. We're both runners."

"I see," Cole said, nodding. "What brought you to Austin?"

"Business," Griff replied. "How about them Cowboys?"

J.J. hooted with laughter. "He gotcha good, big brother. How about them Cowboys?"

Cole frowned. "Was I making you uncomfortable, Griff? Sorry. To tell you the truth, I never cared much for the

Cowboys. I was an Oilers man until they moved to Tennessee and changed their name. You a football fan?"

"More baseball than football."

"Okay, guys," Belle said. "Break it up. We're not going to have any of that men-huddled-around-the-beer stuff. Mix and mingle. Who thinks they could beat me at a game of horse-shoes before lunch?"

"Ding-a-ling," Cole said, throwing an arm around her neck in a headlock. "I can whip you any day of the week."

Saved by the bell, Griff thought, wandering off to find Cass. He met Skye and Flora, the artist, a slightly fey woman in a purple outfit who studied him intently. She cocked her head this way and that, then said, "Ah, you have an interesting aura. I'd like to talk with you more later." She patted his cheek and sighed.

When Flora flitted away, Griff asked Cass, "What did she mean?"

Skye chuckled. "With Mother, one never knows. She sees things some of the rest of us don't, and she's always looking for subjects to paint. I have a lovely painting of Sam in armor and wearing his cowboy hat. She nailed him perfectly."

Griff tried not to squirm. Cass's family made him very un-comfortable. Everyone except Gabe. And maybe Belle and Nonie. Griff gravitated toward Gabe, and they discussed the real estate business in the area. He was obviously an astute businessman.

Their picnic lunch was laid out buffet style, and they sat at folding tables under the canopy instead of on blankets. Except for the children. They insisted on sitting among the flowers to eat.

When they finished eating, Wes Outlaw rose. He held his wineglass high. "I'd like to propose a toast to Belle and Gabe and to Skye and Sam on the occasion of their anniversary. May their lives always be as happy as Nonie's and mine have been."

"Hear! Hear!" Everyone raised their glasses.

"Anyone have any announcements to make?" Wes asked, looking around expectantly.

Sunny raised her hand. "Ben and I are getting married in early summer. You'll all be invited."

Everybody cheered and clapped, and J.J. whistled.

Skye raised her hand, and Sam looked at her strangely. "We're expecting a little bundle at our house."

Sam's eyes bugged, and he almost fell off his chair. "We are?"

She laughed. "Our llama's pregnant."

Chapter Six

"Wasn't that fun?" Cass asked on the drive home. "I do adore that bunch of people."

"Nice folks," Griff said.

Even though he smiled and said the right things, Cass got the sudden impression that poor Griff hadn't had fun at all. He'd been charming to everyone the whole afternoon, but was it all an act? "I suppose the gang might be overwhelming all at once. What was I thinking to put you through such an ordeal? Will you forgive me?"

"There's nothing to forgive. I enjoyed meeting your family. I don't recall ever being around so many lawmen at one time—at least not since the cops raided a frat party when I was in college."

"Don't tell me you were intimidated."

"By a forest of drawling Texas Rangers and country sheriffs? Not me, darlin'."

Cass frowned. Did she hear a smidgen of condescension in his tone? More than a smidgen, she decided. And it rankled. She was nuts about her newfound Outlaw relatives and proud of every one of them. Totally aggravated by his attitude, she was tempted to stop her car and leave him on the side of the road. The sooner she could get back to Austin and dump this New Yawk Yankee, the better. She should never have taken up with him in the first place. A cute butt and gorgeous eyes didn't trump narrow-mindedness.

Griff must have picked up on her thoughts because he said, "Okay, I admit the Outlaw guys made me a little uneasy. The mere size of them is enough to make anybody quake in their boots."

"But they're all pussycats. Sweet as pie."

Griff chuckled. "Don't let the big grins and back slapping fool you. Those guys, McKee included, could wade into a pack of hungry grizzlies and come out unscathed."

Cass laughed. "And with several bearskin rugs. I'll give you that."

"I wouldn't want to meet any of them in a dark alley. I'm a lover, not a fighter." He gave her a very engaging grin.

She laughed again. She suspected that Griffin Mitchell could hold his own in that alley, but his comments had deflated her pique with him. "Don't discount Belle. She has a black belt in something or other."

"I'm not at all surprised. Are you a martial arts expert, as well?"

Cass rolled her eyes. "Hardly. Now Sunny is another story. She's the tough twin."

"What was your father like?" Griff asked. "Was he as big as the rest of the Outlaws?"

"I never saw him." She wasn't going to mention the recent glimpses she'd had of the Senator—or whoever. "I gather from talking with Uncle Wes that they were about the same size—about like J.J. when they were young."

"You and Sunny look a great deal like your cousin Belle."

"Everybody says that. Strong Outlaw genes, I suppose."

"You must be tired," Griff said. "Would you like me to drive?"

She grinned. "Is that a subtle hint for me to ease up on the accelerator?"

"Not at all. Just an offer."

"I'm fine. I love driving. I missed not having a car when I was in New York. I tried keeping one for a while, but the parking was ridiculous and the traffic so unbelievable I gave up after a couple of months. Do you have a car?"

"I keep one at my parents' house, but I live in Manhattan and travel so much it's not practical for me to have one in the city. If I decide to move to Austin, I'll have to have a car. Around here, it's a necessity."

"For sure."

As they neared his hotel, he said, "I noticed in the newspaper this morning that *Butch Cassidy and the Sundance Kid* is showing at some place called the Alamo Drafthouse. Know where it is?"

"Of course. It's a movie theater with some added features—like beer and food. There are several around town. They show old movies as well as first runs. Sometimes there's live entertainment."

"Would you like to go see Butch and Sundance jump off the cliff?"

She thought for a moment, testing for any residual irritation with him. Not finding any and not having anything better to do, she said, "Sure." She checked her watch. "I suspect the evening feature will be starting soon."

"I hope we have time to change and still make it."

"Change? Change what?"

"Our clothes. I have grass stains all over my shorts."

She laughed. "Griff, are you ever going to learn? Trust me,

nobody at the Alamo will notice. Though you might fit in better if you had some flip-flops."

"Can we at least stop by my hotel and let me wash up?"

"Well, I suppose. If you insist."

CASS WASN'T SO SURE stopping by his hotel suite was the brightest decision she ever made. Feeling tired, she plopped down on the comfy couch while he went into the bedroom. He left the door open, and she could see the king-size bed and a shirt he'd tossed on it.

Funny how a casually dropped shirt could stir sensual little shivers in her. She'd never met a man who could turn her on— and off—so easily. One minute she wanted to jump his bones and the next she wanted to brain him with the nearest blunt object. Was her seesawing a result of fighting her attraction to him? Maybe so, but at the moment the switch was flipped to On.

She hugged her knees and curled up on the couch, leaning her head back against the soft pillow. Was any sort of relationship with Griff worth pursuing? He might be gone to who knows where next week. But the fact was, she had a powerful itch for the man. On the other hand, he had a lot in common with Daniel, her ex-fiancé, and that was scary.

Cass sighed, and her next breath drew in his scent, a sexy male aroma totally different from Daniel's. Her hormones began to dance like dervishes.

He came out a moment later, hair brushed and fresh shorts on.

"Did you think I wouldn't notice?" she asked.

"Notice what?"

"That you changed your clothes. The grass stains are gone."

He grinned. "You don't miss much, do you?"

"Nope."

"The grass stains were bad enough, but some other unknown substance was a little sticky. Will you forgive me if I promise to buy some flip-flops tomorrow?"

"It's a deal," she said. "May I use your bathroom for a minute?"

"Of course. I'll check the paper for the starting time."

Using his bathroom wasn't the smartest thing Cass ever did. His scent surrounded her, tantalizing her as she freshened her makeup and brushed out her hair. She washed her hands and made a quick retreat.

Still, the moment she saw him sitting on the couch and studying the paper, she had the strongest urge to snatch away the entertainment section and pin him to the cushions.

She restrained herself.

"We've got twenty minutes to get there," he said. "Think we can make it?"

"If we jog, we can be there in five minutes. Race you." She turned and bolted.

"You're on," he said, slamming his hand against the door before she could open it. "The race starts outside."

Downstairs, he politely allowed her to pass through the automatic doors ahead of him, but she didn't wait for a starting gun. She was off.

Griff caught up easily, but stayed beside her as they jogged down the wide sidewalk that led to the capitol building on the hill.

They turned on Sixth Street and stopped in front of an old movie theater in the nightclub-restaurant area. Cass was breathing hard, but Griff wasn't even winded. Irritating.

"Is this it?"

"This is it."

He patted his back pocket, then scowled. "Damn. I left my wallet in my other shorts. Wait here and I'll run back for it."

"No need. I have my emergency fund." She pulled out the small folder that held her driver's license, a credit card and a hundred-dollar bill. "Tonight's on me."

"Do you have enough to buy a hot dog? I'm hungry."

"M'dear, I have plenty, but let's have something better than a hot dog. The Alamo Drafthouse is literally a dinner theater. We can have a full meal while we watch the movie."

"Really?"

"Yep." She bought their tickets, and they went inside. "This one is the Alamo Ritz, named after the original theater."

The place was laid out like a regular cinema except that every other row of seats had been removed and replaced with a long table. They found a spot easily enough, and Cass joined in the sing-along being conducted from the stage. She hadn't been here in ages, and she'd always adored the place.

Griff looked through the menu. "What's good here?"

"Just about everything. I've always loved their appetizers. Want to start with some nachos and frozen margaritas?"

"Sure. How about some wings, too?"

"Sounds good."

After they ordered, Cass goaded him into singing along with the crowd. Actually, he had a very nice baritone voice, and soon he was belting out "I'm an old cowhand…" while they put their heads together and harmonized.

While they watched Butch and Sundance, they drank margaritas, munched on nachos, wings and fish tacos, and yelled out, along with the crowd, the most famous lines in the script or comments to the screen characters.

This was the Austin she loved.

WHEN THE FILM WAS OVER, they walked back to Griff's hotel arm in arm, laughing and talking about the movie and the whole day.

"I don't remember when I've had so much fun as I've had this trip to Austin," Griff said.

"And why is that?" Cass asked with an exaggerated fluttering of her eyelashes.

He grinned and tousled her hair. "I think you've had a lot to do with that. And I do love this town. My blood pressure must have dropped twenty points since I stepped off the plane at Bergstrom Airport."

"I can relate to that. New York is a nice place to visit, but I'll always want to live in Austin. There's something in the air that makes it special. I think the reason we've grown so much in the past few years is students and visitors who come to town never want to leave. We have lots of waiters in town with master's degrees."

When they arrived at his hotel, Griff asked, "Want to come up?"

"I'll have to. I left my purse in your room." *Freudian slip?* she wondered.

Of course not, her practical side said.

Of course, her libido declared.

After Griff unlocked his door, he asked, "Shall I order up a bottle of wine, or do you want to check the mini fridge first?"

Dare she stay for a drink? The smart thing to do would be to grab her purse and hotfoot it home.

Chapter Seven

Maybe it would be smart to leave, but Cass's credo had always asserted smart wasn't always the most fun. She had a powerful yen for Griffin Mitchell, and the margaritas had dulled her inhibitions. This might be the perfect opportunity to discover if he was everything her imagination had him cracked up to be.

Of course, all she could think of on the way up in the elevator was that she'd been tromping around in the bluebonnets half the day, gorging on Mexican food, and probably smelled worse than a goat. She couldn't quite say, *Hey, if we're going to have a romp in the hay, could I take a shower and brush my teeth first?*

Or could she?

No way. She was a modern woman, but she wasn't *that* modern. She'd always been too cautious for casual sex. And, truthfully, she was a closet romantic. It had been a long time since she'd had sex of any kind. She hadn't met anybody who'd lit her boilers until Griff came along.

"You're very quiet," he said. "Tired?"

"No. In fact, I'm kind of jazzed."

"Me, too. I was just thinking a dip in the pool would feel

great. Too bad you don't have a suit. I wonder if the gift shop downstairs has any?"

Perfect solution to her dilemma, Cass thought. A nice swim, a shower…*ahhh.* "I'm sure they do."

"Let's check." When the elevator door opened on his floor, Griff punched the button down to the lobby.

In the gift shop, he zeroed on a red patterned bikini. Cass checked the tag. It was her size, but the price on it was ridiculous.

He must have caught her frown. "My treat," he said. "Payback for the day."

She didn't argue. Nor did she protest when he handed a matching cover-up and slides to the clerk and charged the purchase to his room. After all, she suspected Griff could easily afford it. If he'd been on a budget, he would have been at Motel 6 instead of in a lake-view suite at the most expensive hotel in town. Too, she thought, he was macho enough to want to make up for her having to foot the bill for the evening's expenses. Men were sometimes goofy like that.

Back upstairs, he insisted that she take the bathroom while he changed in the living room. Cass took time for a quick shower and put on her new suit. It was a perfect fit, but a tiny bit of her appendectomy scar showed. Although it had faded considerably since she was fourteen and she rarely thought about it, she was suddenly very self-conscious. Why hadn't she chosen a one-piece as she usually did?

She sighed. Oh well. If a scar turned Griff off, so be it. What was, was. She pulled on her cover-up, stepped into her slides and grabbed a couple of towels and terry robes as she left the bathroom.

Griff smiled when she came out. "Ready?"

"Yep. Let's hit that pool."

They went down the elevator again.

"I heard you taking a shower," he said. "I must smell like a goat."

She giggled—and couldn't stop. They'd both had goats on their mind.

"Am I really that bad?" he asked.

"Not at all."

"Then what's so funny?"

Cass giggled again. "I'd been thinking the same thing about me earlier."

He threw an arm around her neck and gave her a peck on the nose. "You certainly don't smell like a goat. You smell like…bluebonnets."

"For your information, bluebonnets don't smell."

He grinned. "Neither do you."

"Is the pool indoor or outdoor?"

"Outdoor, but it's heated so the water should be perfect."

And it was. The full moon shimmered over the lake, just visible between the trees lining the shore, and sparkled on the surface of the pool.

"It's like swimming in moonbeams," Cass said as she did a slow breaststroke across the water.

"I arranged it just for you," Griff said, pacing himself beside her.

She laughed. "Yeah, sure. But it is nice. And we have the whole pool to ourselves." She glanced up at the bank of hotel windows. "And whoever is playing voyeur inside."

She changed to a fast crawl, and still Griff kept pace. When she reached the edge of the pool, she grabbed on and wiped the water from her face.

"You're a regular otter," he said, catching hold with both hands so that she was pinned.

"I love swimming, but I haven't had much opportunity lately. This is a fantastic pool."

"You're welcome to come anytime you'd like." He moved his face closer to hers, then touched her lips with his.

Desire shot through her. If she'd done what she wanted to, they would probably have drowned. Plus the voyeurs would have had an eyeful.

His tongue played over her lips and the pressure of his mouth deepened. Maybe drowning wasn't such a bad way to go, and to hell with whoever was watching. Her arms went around his neck, her legs around his waist, and she returned his kiss with all the pent-up passion in her. Warm morphed into scorching until she was sure the water around her boiled.

He groaned and reached for the ties to her bikini top. She clung tighter to him.

"Ahem!" a voice said. "Ahem!"

They both looked up to see a man standing nearby. "I'm sorry, but the pool is closing."

"But we just got here," Griff said, his voice hoarse.

"Sorry, sir, but it's eleven o'clock. Perhaps you would be more comfortable…in your room." The attendant grinned and winked.

Cass felt herself turn a thousand shades of red. What in the world was she thinking? That was the problem. She hadn't been thinking. Another couple of minutes and she'd have been stripped in front of God and everybody.

"I could die," she murmured.

"Don't do that," Griff whispered. "I have better things in mind, and I'm not into necrophilia."

She made sure her bikini top was tied, and hoisted herself from the pool. They quickly rinsed off, toweled themselves dry and donned terry robes. Cass barely had time to step into her slides before Griff grabbed her hand and dragged her inside.

In the empty elevator he took her into his arms again, and she melted like warm chocolate against him. Every cell in her body was on high alert. Her brain was a bowl of tapioca, and she ached with yearning. She'd never felt so out of control. She didn't care if she barely knew this man; she only cared that she wanted him in the worst way. Longing filled her mind and throbbed in her body. Reason was overwhelmed by primal urges stronger than anything she'd ever experienced before. For once, she didn't want to *think;* she wanted to *feel.* She needed to feel again.

When the bell dinged, Griff seemed to come to his senses enough to exit and pull her after him. He fumbled with the key card until the door opened. Robes and bathing suits went flying, and they barely made it to the couch before Griff was on top of her, kissing, caressing, moaning. She responded to his every move, frantic with desire, urging him to enter.

"Wait, wait!" he said. "Don't move. I'll be right back."

Cass protested, but he jumped over the back of the couch and returned in mere seconds, rolling on a condom. He knelt between her legs, scooped up her bottom and plunged deep inside. She screamed as he entered, and a powerful orgasm racked her immediately. "Oh, hell. Did I hurt you?"

"Not…hardly," she gasped, as the spasms seemed to go on forever.

"That was something new for me."

"Thank God." He gave a second thrust and stiffened with his own release.

In a few moments, he withdrew and repositioned them so he lay on the couch and cuddled her on top of him.

"I can't believe…" she murmured. "I'm usually not…"

"Not what?"

"So…uh…quick to become aroused and…well, you seem to do strange things to me."

He squeezed her against him. "I can usually control myself a little better, too. Woman, you turn me on like crazy. I've had the hots for you since the first time I laid eyes on you."

"Really?"

"Really. Do you have to work tomorrow?"

She shook her head.

"Good. We can spend the rest of the night and all day tomorrow taking it a little slower."

"All night and all day? We'll be exhausted. Do you think you can last that long?"

He chuckled. "I'd sure as hell like to try."

Cass took another shower and washed and dried her hair while Griff ordered a bottle of wine and late night snacks.

They drank wine and watched TV and made love again on the couch. Slowly. It was lovely.

They slept and he awakened her with kisses, and they made love again. Slowly. It was even lovelier.

Cass stirred when she felt kisses moving up and down her spine.

"It's morning," Griff whispered. "Want some breakfast?"

"Coffee."

"Anything else?" he asked.

"You choose. I'm sleepy."

He kissed her shoulder and chuckled. "Go back to sleep. I'll wake you when food comes."

She dozed for a few minutes, then blinked herself awake, dragged herself out of the big bed and into the bathroom, which was still steamy from Griff's shower. Showering again, Cass dried off, then realized she didn't have any clean clothes.

Wrapping herself in a towel, she searched the closet and found a blue dress shirt. From in the dresser she helped herself to a pair of knit boxer briefs.

Just as she did up the last button, Griff tapped lightly on the door.

"Breakfast."

She opened it. "I raided your clothes."

"Help yourself. My shirt never looked so good."

He grinned, and she wanted to grab on to him like a monkey and never let go. What was the matter with her? She'd never acted this way before or felt like this about any man. This was crazy. And scary. She ought to run for the hills, but she wasn't going anywhere until she had a major jolt of caffeine.

Griff waved a cup under her nose, and she followed the heavenly scent of coffee like a bloodhound as he enticed her to the lavishly set table.

"Gimme, gimme!" She grabbed for the cup, but he held it up over her head. "I've been known to kill for less," she growled.

"Yours is poured and waiting by your plate."

Downing half a cup immediately, she sighed. "Heavenly. Thank you, sir."

"You're very welcome, madam." He began lifting plate covers. "French toast. Eggs, bacon, sausages. Cereal. Fruit. Anything here tickle your fancy?"

Looking him up and down, she cocked an eyebrow.

He grinned. "The food, I mean."

"All of it. I'm starved."

When she had polished off a good portion of the meal and half the coffee, he said, "Shall I order more?"

"Nope." She patted her tummy. "I'm full for now."

She heard the familiar ring tone of her cell phone and

looked around searching for her purse. Griff finally retrieved it from underneath a couch cushion and handed it to her.

"It's Sunny," she told him. "Hi, sis. What's up?"

"Where are you?" Sunny asked.

"I'm having breakfast with a friend."

"Well, get over to Chili Witches right away. We've got a problem."

Chapter Eight

"Where are my clothes?" Cass asked. "I've got to go home pronto."

"I sent them to the laundry," Griff said. "They should be back in a couple of hours. Is there a problem with Sunny?"

"Yes, and it must be serious. She's usually pretty unflappable. I can't go traipsing through the lobby in your shirt and underwear, and I have to leave. Where's my bathing suit?"

"The laundry."

"You sent a *bathing suit* to the laundry?" She rolled her eyes. "Have you ever heard of tossing such things over a shower rod? What am I going to wear home?" She eyed the draperies, but decided against the Scarlett O'Hara solution. "Oh, hell's bells!" She located her sneakers in the bedroom and was tying them on when Griff came in the room.

"I'm sorry, Cass. I thought we were going to spend the day here. Give me a few minutes, and I'll run downstairs to the gift shops and find something suitable."

"Forget it. At those prices, I'd rather endure a little embarrassment. If Leslie can run around town in a sequined bikini, I can wear your shirt and underwear."

"Who's Leslie?"

"He's a local character." She rolled up her sleeves and grabbed her purse. "Have you got a hat?"

He handed her a golf cap, and she crammed it on her head, put on her sunglasses and pecked him on the cheek as she flew toward the door.

"Call me later," he yelled after her as she went out.

Nobody looked at her strangely as she walked through the lobby—or if they did she didn't notice. Folks probably thought she was one of the Hollywood types who frequently came to town for some event or the other.

Cass retrieved her car and sped toward home. The café was surrounded by police cars, utility trucks and even a fire truck. She screeched to a stop down the block and bolted for the back lot, where she saw Sunny talking to a uniformed cop.

"What's going on?" Cass asked.

"Everything is flooded," her sister said, "and the place is a mess."

"Oh my gawd! What happened?"

"We don't know yet," Sunny told her. "Did you notice anything strange going on last night?"

"I—uh—wasn't here last night."

"Hmm." Sunny looked her up and down. "Interesting outfit."

Cass refused to blush. "Let me go upstairs and change, and we'll get this sorted out."

She hurried up to her apartment. Except for her water and electricity being off, everything seemed normal. After quickly changing into jeans and a tee, she rejoined her sister in the back lot.

"Did Hank notice anything unusual?" Cass asked. Hank was a cop friend of Sunny's who lived in the other upstairs apartment, the one where Sunny had lived until she bought her house.

Her twin shook her head. "He spent the night with his fiancée."

"Well, damn."

"Exactly."

"Why are all these people here?" Cass asked.

"Because when I got here a few minutes ago, the alarm was turned off, and water was ankle-deep inside. I didn't want to electrocute myself. Are you sure you set the alarm Saturday night?"

"Of course I'm sure! Do you think I left a faucet running, too?"

"Don't get your panties in a wad, Cass. I was just asking to be sure. I'm hoping this was an accident."

Cass's brows went up. "You mean you think it wasn't? Is anything missing?"

"I don't know yet. People are checking everything out. It might have been a break-in. It might have been a burst pipe and a short in the electrical system. I don't even know how bad the damage is."

"Well, hell," Cass said.

"That, too. We'll just have to wait until all these people have time to investigate and assess the situation."

Sid and Foster, the middle-aged owners of Hooks, the seafood restaurant next door, walked up. "Have they found the source of the problem yet?" Sid asked.

"Not that I've heard," Cass said. "Do you have any damage?"

"Only a few damp spots in the kitchen," Foster, who was the restaurant chef, told them. "I didn't think anything about it when I first noticed. We have a good drainage system."

"So do we," Sunny said. "Or at least I thought so. I can't imagine what happened. We have everybody from the water department and plumbers to the security company, firemen and cops trying to assess the situation. I'm sending our employees home for the day. No way can we serve customers."

"Why don't you girls come next door for a cup of coffee," Sid said.

"Thanks, Sid," Sunny replied, "but I really don't want to leave right now."

"We'll send you out something," Foster said. "I need to get back to the kitchen."

A few minutes later a waiter and a busboy from Hooks brought out a table and set up a coffee and water station in the parking lot. One of their neighbors, who had stopped by to see what the fuss was about, brought over a plastic tub of cookies for the table. Everything was soon scarfed up by the various people on site, including the media reporters who stopped by for the story.

After what seem like forever, the consensus seemed to be that the back door lock had been jimmied and either someone forgot to set the alarm or someone knew the code. In an act of malicious mischief, the someone or someones had deliberately stopped up the drains and turned on every water faucet in the kitchen and bathrooms. Nothing seemed to be missing.

"Who would do such a thing?" Cass asked.

"Beats me," Sunny said, "and the chances of ever catching them are somewhere between slim and none. I don't think I've pissed off anybody lately. Have you?"

"Not that I can think of. Our problem now is cleaning up the mess. Have you called the insurance adjuster?"

"He's on his way, and as soon as he takes a look at things, we need to start cleaning and assessing damage," Sunny said.

"I vote for calling in the professionals," Cass said. "There are companies that specialize in stuff like this. What are we going to do about all the food in the cooler and freezer?"

"Oh, Lord. What a mess."

THE FOOD, WHICH WAS deemed safe, they gave to various homeless shelters and kitchens, and decided to leave the cleanup to professionals, as Cass had suggested. While she was packing a bag to move to Sunny's house for a couple of days, Griff phoned.

"Is everything okay?" he asked.

"No. Everything has been chaos here. I'm sorry I forgot to call you." She told him about the break-in and damages to Chili Witches.

"Where are you?" he asked.

"In my apartment."

"I'll be right there."

Before she could say more, he was gone. She locked up, went downstairs and stowed her bag in her car. There were a million and one details to tend to, not the least of which were calling their mom and Aunt Min and telling them about the incident.

"I've been thinking," Sunny said as they stood watching the water being pumped out. "Maybe it would be a good idea to wait a few days before calling Mom and Aunt Min. By next week, everything ought to be back to normal."

"That's a brilliant idea. I'm for it." They grinned at each other. "They're such worriers."

No sooner were the words out of her mouth than Cass's cell rang. She glanced at the ID screen and frowned. "Who else do we know in France?"

Sunny groaned. "We never have been able to get away with anything."

"Hi, Mom," Cass said.

"Cassidy," her mother stated. "What's going on there? Min and I have been worried all day, and nobody is answering the phone at Chili Witches. I know something is wrong. Is Sunny sick?"

"No, Mom. Nothing like that. She's fine. In fact, she's standing right here beside me. You want to talk to her?"

Sunny held up her hands and began shaking her head. "You tell her," she whispered.

"Uh, Mom, we've just had a little plumbing problem here, and we're having to close down a couple of days to get it fixed."

"What kind of problem?" her mother asked. "Now, don't beat around the bush, Cassidy. Tell me all of it."

Cass rolled her eyes and told her the whole story.

"Oh, my stars and garters! I was afraid something like this would happen. Min and I will be home on the first plane."

"No, no, Mom. Don't cut your stay short. Everything is under control here. Sunny and I can handle things just fine."

Griff arrived while she was trying to placate her mother, and she could only wave to him and mouth, *"My mom. Just a minute."*

He nodded and went to investigate the situation in the café—as if *he* could do anything that wasn't already being done. By the time she got off the phone and related the conversation to Sunny, Griff was back.

"Looks like they have everything under control. Any idea who would do such a thing?" he asked.

Cass shook her head. "Probably the same kind of goofball who set fire to the governor's mansion a while back. The police seem to think it's malicious mischief, since nothing was stolen. Any available cash—and there wasn't much—is in a big wall safe that would take a stick of dynamite or a blowtorch to open."

"Have you ladies had lunch?"

"No," Sunny said. "I haven't even thought about lunch."

Cass glanced at her watch and was surprised to find it was after two o'clock. "For once I haven't even thought of food."

"How's the restaurant next door?" Griff asked. "Is it open?"

"Hooks is great, but I think we should hang around here for a while," Cass said.

"You two go ahead," Sunny told them, "and I'll stay here."

"Let's all go," Griff said. "I'll tell the crew where we'll be in case you're needed."

Cass wasn't sure if she was grateful or irritated with Griff's taking charge, but her stomach was beginning to rumble, so she let it go.

FOSTER OUTDID HIMSELF on their late lunch, and it was delicious. When Griff tried to pay the bill, Sid refused his card.

"These girls are like our nieces," he said. "We're devastated about what happened. How long do you think you'll be closed?"

"We're hoping to be open by the weekend," Sunny said. "It depends on how long things take to dry out and how much damage there is to the floor. The company we've called in to restore the place got right on it, so we're hoping the quick response helps."

"Let us know if there's anything we can do," Sid told her.

"Will do. Thanks for the lunch."

"Our pleasure."

After they left, Griff said to Cass, "You obviously can't stay in your apartment yet. I'd like you to stay at my hotel."

"Thanks, Griff, but I'm staying with Sunny—at least for a couple of days. We have a ton of details to attend to, but I appreciate the offer."

He grinned. "It wasn't totally selfless. How can I help you?"

"There's really not anything you can do at the moment."

"Did you have insurance?"

"Yes, and the rep has already been here. Everything's covered—or at least the majority of the damage. Mostly the whole thing is a big pain in the tokus. Thanks for coming by, Griff." She gave him a peck on the cheek.

"Am I being given my hat?" he asked.

She chuckled. "Not exactly, but Sunny and I have a lot to do. We have to talk to our suppliers and put an ad in the paper and…"

"I got it. Call me if there's anything I can do. I'll talk to you tonight."

"Tomorrow might be better."

He nodded and left.

GRIFF GRIPPED THE WHEEL of his rental car a little too tightly as he drove back to his hotel. Ever since he learned about the damage to Chili Witches, he'd had a niggling feeling about it. This smelled of Walt, one of Griff's partners. Maybe he was wrong. Maybe this was a coincidence, but he wouldn't put it past the guy. Walt was a brilliant businessman, but he was impatient and impulsive. And a master of dirty tricks. His partners wanted that property yesterday. Griff had asked them repeatedly to be patient and let him handle things his way.

As soon as he got to his hotel, he whipped out his phone and punched the speed dial. Walt answered immediately.

"Walt, did you have anything to do with Chili Witches flooding?"

He chuckled. "Me? Now would I do something so appalling?"

"Hell, yes. In a heartbeat. Back off, Walt."

Chapter Nine

Cass was bone tired when she drove to Sunny's house that evening; she literally ached and her head felt as if dirt daubers were building nests inside. She pulled into the driveway behind her sister, who trudged toward the door as if she could barely put one foot in front of the other. With the stress and the mess and the mountain of things to do, it had been a killer of a day. Cass hauled her bag from the trunk and trudged inside in the same manner.

They both headed straight for the couch, plopped down and rested their heads against the cushioned back. Leo, Sunny's German shepherd, joined them, nuzzling against Sunny's leg.

"I may die," Cass said.

"Please don't," Sunny said, absently stroking Leo's head. "I'm too tired to plan your funeral."

Cass laughed, then they both got the giggles. The giggles turned into tears. They held each other and wept from exhaustion and despair.

After they had a good cry, Sunny wiped her nose and said, "Do you ever wonder exactly why we do this?"

"What? Cry? I think it's supposed to release some sort of

chemicals to make you feel better." Cass fished a tissue from her purse and blew her nose.

"No, I mean why are we working so hard to keep Chili Witches going? Sometimes I feel the café has become the center of my life. How did Mom and Aunt Min do it for all those years?"

"Beats me. I suppose because they loved the place. I never figured I'd end up running it, but let me tell you, it's better than being a lawyer in New York. Do you hate managing the café?"

"No, I don't hate it. In fact, most of the time I enjoy it, but the hours are hard—and will be harder after Ben and I get married. There's Jay to think of, and I'd like to have children someday. I don't want to raise them in a playpen in the office or put them in day care and only see them half the week."

"We were lucky to have Aunt Min and Mom when we were growing up. It was like having two mothers," Cass said, "but don't count on me to babysit. Aunt Min I ain't."

"You don't want children?" Sunny asked.

"Do you see me as the domestic type?"

"I don't know. Maybe. We're a lot alike, and I can feel the ticking biological clock everybody's always talking about."

Cass rolled her eyes. "The only clock I feel ticking is the one signaling dinnertime, but I'm too tired to eat, much less cook."

"I hear that."

The doorbell rang.

"I wonder who that could be?" Sunny glanced over her shoulder. "Want to get the door?"

"*Moi?* Surely you jest. Nobody knows I'm here, and I wouldn't get up and go to the door for the Publisher's Clearing House prize van."

Sunny groaned and heaved herself from the couch. "Whoever it is better not be selling magazines."

It was Ben McKee with food his sister had sent over. "I'm not staying," Cass heard him say. "I know you must be tired, and Jay's waiting in the car. I'll call later. Or better, you call me when it's convenient."

Sunny came back with a big bag, which she deposited on the coffee table. "I'll get plates and forks while I'm up. Check out the contents."

Cass was just opening the sack when the doorbell rang again.

"Your turn," Sunny called from the kitchen.

Cass muttered a few choice words and plodded to the door. A deliveryman stood on the porch, a large bag stamped with the logo of her favorite Italian restaurant in each hand.

"Cassidy Outlaw?" he asked.

"That's me."

"These are for you from Mr. Mitchell." He handed her the fancy, handled bags. "No tip necessary. Have a good evening."

She closed the door with her butt as Sunny asked, "Who was that?"

"Another care package. This one from Griff."

"Did you invite him in?"

"The deliveryman? Nope. Not my type. He had a nose ring."

"Oh, well, add it to the bounty on the coffee table, and we'll have a buffet. What do you want to drink?"

"I think there's a bottle of wine in one of these bags," Cass said. "Bring glasses and a corkscrew."

Her cell phone rang as she was unloading all the sacks of food. Griff.

"Hi," she said. "Thanks for the food. It just arrived."

"Good. I wanted to check. I would have delivered it myself, but I doubted you were up to company tonight. I hope you enjoy it. Is there anything I can do to help you?"

"Not that I can think of, but I appreciate the offer."

"I'll drop by the café tomorrow to see if you need anything. Eat and get a good night's sleep."

"Well, bless his sweet heart," Cass whispered as she continued laying out the King Ranch chicken casserole and shrimp Portofino and salads and decadent desserts. "How thoughtful. Maybe there are a few decent New York lawyers, after all."

AS IT TURNED OUT, the tile floors in the bathrooms and kitchen were fine, but those in the serving area and office were a lost cause. Cass and Sunny shopped around and selected a laminate wood floor that looked like old planks and promised to wear like iron. The installers arrived on Thursday to lay down the new surface.

Their mother and Aunt Min were arriving on the same day. The twins had only a few hours notice to air out the town house their mom and aunt shared a few blocks from the café. They called a maid service to clean and change linens. Sunny stocked the pantry while Cass bought flowers and a couple of plants to brighten up the place, which had been closed for months.

Cass placed a vase of irises on the hall table and stepped back to admire them. "I wish we could have talked them out of coming," she said to Sunny. "They were having a wonderful time in France and could have stayed another few weeks at least."

"When have we ever been able to talk those two out of anything? They still think of us as their babies."

Cass sighed. "I know. They worry. What time is their plane due?"

"Three o'clock. We'd better get going. They'll be exhausted, and the time difference is going to be hard on them. I hope they slept some on the plane."

"Fat chance."

They locked up and headed for the airport.

"We got another one of those letters today," Sunny said as they drove.

"What letters?"

"The one from the guy in New York offering us an obscene amount of money for Chili Witches and the surrounding property. He upped his offer by ten percent."

"You're kidding. After my reply to his last offer, I certainly didn't expect to hear from him again. Let's just ignore this one."

"Don't you think we should mention it to Mom and Aunt Min? After all, they're the majority stockholders of the company."

"I suppose so," Cass said, "but you know their answer. They'd sooner sell a kidney than part with Chili Witches. The guy probably wants to raze the buildings and put up offices or, God forbid, another condo high-rise."

"I thought the high-rise craze had passed."

"Nope. Rumor is it's coming back with a vengeance. POAC is a watchdog for irresponsible destruction and building, and we keep our ear to the ground. If we hadn't been on our toes last month, some idiot would have leveled an entire grove of pecan trees and put in a car wash."

"Cass, a car wash is a legitimate business."

"Of course it is, but we worked with the guy to reconfigure his layout and be able to save most of the trees. It not only made for a more attractive place, but now he can also bill his business as eco-friendly, and eco-friendly is in."

"Well, good for POAC," Sunny said. "And good for you, tiger. Sic 'em."

CASS THOUGHT HER MOTHER and aunt had never looked so lovely—even after a grueling overseas flight. Gloria and

Minerva O'Connor weren't twins—Aunt Min was older by a year and a half—but they looked very much alike. Both were still trim and a couple of inches shorter than Sunny and Cass. The streaks of gray in their strawberry-blond hair had disappeared in the months they had been gone, and they both had new short and fashionable haircuts instead of their old styles, which was usually some sort of convenient twist. They both looked ten years younger than their sixty plus.

"You look fantastic," Cass said, hugging her mother, then Aunt Min. "What have you done to yourselves?"

Gloria beamed. "I highly recommend retirement. And the new French makeovers helped." She fluffed her hair. "Like it?"

"I love it. Aunt Min, are you sure you haven't had a face-lift?"

Min chuckled. "Absolutely not, but we went to this lovely salon for skin treatments." She rubbed her cheek. "Soft as a baby's butt. Feel."

"You're right, and you both look so rested. Were you able to sleep on the plane?"

"We were," Gloria said. "You two, on the other hand, look like you've been dragged through a knothole backward. But not to worry, we're here to help handle things."

"There's nothing to handle," Sunny said. "Everything has been dried out and checked out and approved. The new floors are going in today and the contractors are coming tomorrow for some minor repair work."

"What about…?"

"Supplies have been ordered for the kitchen," Cass said, kissing her mother's cheek, "and the cooks and kitchen help are coming in over the weekend to see that everything will be ready for business on Monday."

Gloria looked at Min. "See, I told you our girls could handle the situation."

"Ha!" Min said. "You were chomping at the bit to get here. Same as me. We have Sunny's wedding to plan, anyhow. We just came back a little early."

Sunny sighed. "I've told you. There's nothing to plan. We're going to have a simple wedding with only family and a few friends."

"We'll discuss that later," her mother said, clearly intimating her preference for a more elaborate do. "Even small weddings take preparation. We're eager to meet Ben."

"He's eager to meet you, too," Sunny told her. "He'll probably be over for dinner tonight."

"Good, good," Min said. "Come on. Let's get our bags and stretch our legs. We love Europe, but it's wonderful to be home. I've been dying for a big plate of barbecued ribs. Did you know you can't get a decent barbecued rib in France? For all their culinary expertise, they've never managed to make a good old Texas barbecue sauce."

"Or a good bowl of chili," Gloria said as they walked toward the baggage carousels. "And forget enchiladas. Of course, we could make our own chili and enchiladas, but we didn't have a proper barbecue pit."

Cass laughed. "I'm surprised you didn't build one and open a barbecue joint and a chili parlor."

Gloria and Min glanced at each other. "We've considered it," Min admitted.

"Don't you dare!" Cass said. "You're retired."

Gloria sighed. "I know. And I love having time to paint."

"Tell you what," Sunny said. "Let's get you settled, and you can come over and see my new house tonight and have a big barbecue dinner."

"I'll vote for that," Min said. "That's one of my bags. The one with the red tassel."

After the bags were collected and loaded, the two older women insisted on stopping by the café before they went home. Cass and Sunny were eager to check out things, too, so they made a swing by the place. The assistant manager and two of their waiters were moving chairs and tables back inside from where they'd been stored in Cass's apartment. What wouldn't fit there were in Sunny's garage, courtesy of friends with pickups.

"Oh, I like the new floor," Gloria said.

"So do I," Min added. "The old one had seen better days, anyhow. Was the wiring damaged?"

"Luckily, no," Cass said. "At least nothing major. Everything has been checked out and is working fine. We hired a restoration company who got right on it. They had the water pumped out and the fans going almost immediately. The registers and computer equipment are stashed upstairs in Hank's living room, and Griff hired a moving company to move the office furniture and file cabinets to Sunny's storage unit."

"Who's Griff?" Gloria asked.

Trust her mother's antennae to go up.

"He's a guy I've been dating."

"And why haven't we heard about him before? Is he local?"

"No, Mom, he's not local, and I've only been seeing him for a couple of weeks. It's nothing serious."

Gloria's eyebrow rose, and she glanced at her sister. "What does he do?"

"He's a lawyer."

Gloria's eyebrow went even higher.

GRIFF, THE SWEETHEART, insisted on providing the barbecue dinner. Cass was surprised he didn't suggest having it catered. He'd been überhelpful and attentive during their crisis at Chili

Witches, certainly more solicitous of her than Daniel had ever been—and they'd been engaged. Maybe all New York lawyers weren't tarred with the same brush.

Sunny had invited Ben and Jay over, as well. Their mom and aunt were itching to meet the groom. Cass was sure there wouldn't be any objections to him; Ben McKee was a dear. And she couldn't imagine them not liking Griff as well. He was a first-class charmer.

Chapter Ten

It was Jay who stole the show. Both Gloria and Min fell in love with Ben's little boy, who was especially delightful in relating his Montessori class's trip to a goat farm.

After the men left, Gloria said, "Jay is a little doll. And, Sunny, I like your Ben very much."

"He's a wonderful father and will make a good husband for you," Min said. "He obviously adores you."

Cass waited for comments about Griff, who had been charming and solicitous as usual. None came. She finally said, "Griff was very sweet to provide our dinner."

"Yes, he was," Gloria agreed.

Min began clearing coffee cups. "The ribs were among the best I've ever had. Just suited my taste."

"What did you think of him?" Cass asked directly.

"He has beautiful eyes," her aunt said. "Reminds me a bit of Paul Newman."

Cass had lived with these women long enough to recognize a runaround when she heard it. "But what about him as a person?"

"I don't know him well enough to have an opinion yet," Gloria said, busying herself with cleaning up the remnants of their meal.

"Don't bother with that," Cass said, taking the bowl from her hand. "We'll clean up later. Come on, Mom. Don't dillydally."

"About what?"

Cass chuckled. "About Griff."

"He seems a bit too…"

"Slick," Aunt Min chimed in.

"I was going to say 'prep school,' but that, too."

"Oh, come on, you guys. You've been in France and loved it there. The French wrote the book on snobbery. And Griff's no snob."

"That's only in Paris, and only a few people," Min said. "The French are quite nice folks. And Griff is quite nice, too, I'm sure. We just need to get to know him better. He's not a Texas boy."

"True," Gloria said. She yawned hugely. "My, my, look at the time. I think jet lag is catching up with me."

"Me, too," Min said, managing a yawn of her own. "I think we'd better get along home. We can talk all day tomorrow while we're setting things straight at the café."

AFTER SHE AND SUNNY HAD dropped off their mother and aunt, Cass said, "Obviously Mom and Aunt Min don't like Griff. How do you feel about him?"

"The question isn't how do any of us feel about him. How do you feel about him?"

"I'm not sure. Sometimes I'm crazy about him, and at other times I feel like he's a little too…"

"Slick?"

Cass laughed. "Well, yeah. But I'll tell you this. He's hell on wheels in bed."

"Cass! You haven't already…"

"Yep. I have. And the man turns me on like a house afire."

Sunny chuckled. "There's something to be said about that."

"For sure. And it's not as if we're into any sort of permanent commitment. Griff has made some noises about moving to Austin, but I suspect when his business is finished, he'll hightail it back to New Yawk, and I won't see him again until he's back on business."

"How does that make you feel?"

Cass thought for a minute. "Ambivalent."

"Hmm. Exactly what is Griff's business? I mean, I know he's a lawyer, but what brings him to Austin?"

"I don't know, and he won't say. Confidentiality issues, I assume. I suspect he may be a consultant to some high profile firm or another. Being a lawyer, I understand the need for tight lips, and I haven't pried."

"The cop in me makes me curious."

"I'll admit to a little curiosity of my own. You know, I almost had a heart attack at dinner tonight when Jay said your dog was very much like Dr. Skye's dog."

"Lord, I know," Sunny said. "Ben pulled that one out when he casually mentioned that Dr. Skye was a vet, and changed the subject. I could have kissed him. But, sis, sooner or later, probably sooner, we have to break the news to Mom about meeting the Outlaw relatives. Had any great revelations on just how we're going to broach the subject?"

"Not a one."

"Me, either. And we still have to tell them about the offer on our property, but let's worry about it tomorrow. I'm pooped."

On Friday morning, Cass packed her bag to move back to her apartment and her own bed. All the utilities were on again and the tables and chairs stored there had been moved out. Since the alarm system had been restored and upgraded, and Hank would be next door at night, she didn't have any qualms about staying alone, and she was sure Ben and Sunny would welcome a bit of privacy over the weekend.

Even though she and Sunny had tried to discourage them, her mom and Aunt Min were determined to pitch in at the café to get things up and running. Sunny was taking them by a leasing agency to pick up a car, while Cass went ahead. The new baseboards were almost down by the time she arrived at Chili Witches.

And Griff was there. Looking as if he'd just come off the jogging trail, he smiled when he saw her. "Good morning." He gave her a brief kiss.

"Been out for a run? I've been missing my time on the trail."

"I jogged here instead of around the lake. Thought I'd see if you need me to help with anything. I'm supposed to have a meeting later, but I can reschedule if there's anything I can do for you." He caught her hand and touched it to his lips.

"Nothing, but thanks. The new baseboards look good, don't they?"

"Look fine to me, but I'm no expert on baseboards." He glanced up from where he was nibbling her fingers, and grinned. "I do, however, excel in some other areas. Could I take you away from all this tonight? I can make reservations at Hudson's on the Bend."

"Oh, could you?" She beamed at the mention of the unique restaurant in one of the outlying areas near Lake Travis. "I haven't been there in ages. Are you ready for rattlesnake or wild boar?"

He wiggled his eyebrows slightly. "I'm feeling adventurous, to be sure."

The double entendre wasn't lost on her, and his tongue between her fingers brought a sudden visceral response. "Are you now?"

"I am."

When a throat cleared and a male voice behind her said, "Ma'am?" Cass turned to find one of the carpenters.

She tugged her hand from Griff, and said, "Yes?"

"I have a question about something in the office area."

"I'll be right there." To Griff, she said, "Pick me up here about six-thirty."

"Here?"

"Upstairs in my apartment."

"Do you think staying there is wise?"

"Of course."

He started to say more on the subject, but she was sure her expression stopped him. "Could I mooch some water from you?"

"Sure." Cass pulled a bottle from the cooler, and Griff chugged it down. "Want another for the return trip, or do you want a lift back to the hotel?"

He gave a little twitch of a smile. "Oh, I think those old bones can make it." He kissed her cheek. "See you this evening."

"DAMMIT!" GRIFF SLAMMED down the phone and pulled on his jacket.

Sometimes Walt could be such a jackass. Sometimes? Hell, how about *all* the time. He was getting fed up with his partner. Griff had spent most of the day checking out a couple of sites that would work perfectly well for their building project, both of them cheaper than the O'Connor property appraisal and both available. But for some obscure reason, Walt had his mind set on the Chili Witches site, and Griff was having a hard time trying to steer him in another direction. Not only was the O'Connor property more expensive, Walt had just taken it upon himself to send them a registered letter upping his previous offers. Stupid.

When Griff had said, "Walt, let me handle this in my own way," he'd only laughed in that irritating way he had and remarked that Griff's way didn't seem to be working.

"Dammit!"

He'd hoped to gently bring up the subject of selling the property to Cass after their night together, but the flooding emergency had scotched the plan. He intended to ease into the subject tonight...or tomorrow morning if he got lucky.

He sensed that Sunny would be more amenable to selling out than Cass would. Cass was the one committed to saving old Austin. Their mother and aunt, he wasn't so sure of. The pair of them were sharp old gals. They reminded him of his mother. The whole thing would have to be handled with finesse and not the ham-fisted way Walt worked. Sometimes Griff wondered if Walt wasn't losing it.

When he got back to New York, he was going to call a meeting of the partners and have this out once and for all. Things weren't working lately. Maybe he was simply tired of living out of a suitcase, but as the front man for the firm, travel was a reality of his position. What were his options?

DELIGHTED TO BE BACK in her apartment, Cass dressed for a night out with Griff. She dabbed on a bit of the lovely French scent her mom had brought her, then stepped into her black heels. Just as she gave her outfit a final check, the doorbell rang. Her heart did a little flip, and she had to force herself to walk slowly to the door. She even checked the peephole before she opened it.

It was Griff, looking like a million bucks. Make that ten million.

"You look lovely, dear."

"Thank—" *Ohmygawd!* Her heart almost flew from her chest. Who said that? She hadn't even opened the door.

Standing stiff and still as a post, she closed her eyes and refused to look behind her. She almost hoped it was a burglar; the other alternative was scarier. Unable to stand it a moment longer, she opened one eye and peeked over her shoulder.

There *he* stood. Tall, gray-haired and smiling. Her heart hammered faster.

"You!" she croaked.

"Me."

"But—but—but you can't be there."

He chuckled. "I can't?"

The doorbell rang again. She glanced at the door, then back over her shoulder. He was gone.

Quickly, she unlocked the door and yanked it open.

Griff's smile faded. "What's the matter? You look as if you've seen a ghost."

Cass must have gone a shade paler. She couldn't have had much blood left in her face. "Come in. I'm not quite ready." She turned and fled toward the bathroom.

Shaking and feeling a bit queasy, she propped herself against the vanity and stared at herself in the mirror. She did look as if she'd seen a ghost. Well, she had. Or had she? She splashed water on her face and buried it in a towel. Making an effort to clear her mind, she focused on deep breathing, the kind she'd learned in yoga classes.

Fatigue, she told herself. Fatigue had her mind playing tricks. *Cool it, Cassidy.* She did some more deep breathing until the shaking stopped. When she was calm, she repaired her makeup and added an extra dash of blush.

Pasting a bright smile on her face, she went back to the living room. "Sorry to keep you waiting."

"It was worth it. You look fantastic. Want to order a pizza and stay in?"

"No way. My mouth is watering for diamond-back rattle-snake cakes." Picking up her big purse, she took Griff's arm and steered him to the door.

Although it was a half hour drive to the restaurant, the route was one of the prettiest in Austin. A bit after seven they pulled to a stop in the lot of the restored rock cottage with a huge Texas flag displayed on the wall between the blue-shuttered windows. The fragrance of its beautiful flower and herb gardens filled the evening air.

"Want to sit inside or out on the patio?" Griff asked.

"Inside I think."

The restaurant was a cozy and colorful mixture of rustic and elegant, and the tables were set with crisp white cloths and gleaming glasses and tableware.

When they were seated and looked at the menu, Griff said, "You weren't kidding about the rattlesnake."

"Nope. They have lots of exotic dishes here, and if venison, quail or wild boar doesn't suit you, they have tamer things like ordinary steak and lobster. And their wine list is extensive."

"Are you up to trying the chef's seven-course meal?" Griff asked. "I don't believe I've ever had seven courses before. Five maybe."

"Go for it," Cass said. "I don't think I could eat that much, and I don't much care for duck."

"I love duck. What looks good to you?"

"I think I'm going to ask the chef for his recommendation."

"You know the chef here?"

"Of course. Where do you think he comes for chili?"

The chef did indeed have suggestions, and they had a fabulous meal.

"Now I can say I've eaten rattlesnake," Griff said.

"Think anybody in New Yawk will be impressed?"

"Cass, what is it with you and New York? You must have really been stung there. Was it a man?"

"Only partly. That was the final straw." She stared into her wineglass and moved it in a slow circle. "It's a matter of 'New York is a great place to visit, but I wouldn't want to live there.' And even though I was fairly successful, I really wasn't cut out to be a lawyer. I suppose that because Sunny and I were raised with the Outlaw myth of everybody in the family choosing an occupation in law and law enforcement, we naturally gravitated in that direction."

"And now you sell chili."

She laughed. "And now we sell chili."

"Ever thought of franchising the place? I think Chili Witches would go over great in New York. And Chicago. And Denver."

"Sunny and I have talked about it, but we've never gone beyond the talking stage. We've also given some thought to a company that wants to offer a frozen version commercially."

"Sounds like a great idea," Griff said. "Who was the man?"

She frowned. "Who wanted to market frozen chili?"

He shook his head. "No, the man in New York."

"Just another attorney with my firm." She shrugged. "We were engaged, but that didn't stop him from throwing me under the bus to score points with the bosses. I trusted him, and he used me."

"I'm sorry." Griff looked pained, and she wanted to hug him for his sensitivity. "What did he do?"

She signed. "I really don't want to talk about it. I'd much rather have dessert. What looks good to you?"

He grinned, cocked an eyebrow and stared across the table at her.

Cass returned his grin with a cheeky one of her own. "Besides that?"

They decided on coffee outside on the patio, and had their dessert boxed up to take home. When they were the only two left outside under the stars and full moon, the waiter removed their cups, and they strolled through the garden.

Cass breathed in the lovely fragrance of geraniums and roses mixed with herbs. "Isn't it wonderful out here?" she asked.

He nodded. "I really like Austin."

"Because of the great food?"

He took her in his arms and kissed her. "That, too. I can hardly wait for dessert."

Chapter Eleven

On the way back to town, they debated about going to Cass's apartment or to Griff's hotel. "I vote for your hotel," she said. "That way I don't run the risk of your running into my relatives on your way out."

Griff chuckled. "And you're how old?"

"Don't hand me that, smart guy. Would you have a woman over if you knew your mother was dropping by for breakfast?"

"Point taken. My mother is a bit old-fashioned."

"And despite the circumstances of Sunny's and my birth— or maybe because of it—so is mine. She likes to think Sunny and I are still virgins."

He laughed. "But I thought you told me Sunny's been married."

"So?"

"My hotel it is. Have you told your mom about meeting the Outlaws yet?"

"Not yet. Sunny and I are trying to think of the best way to break it gently."

"Better hurry or they'll find out some other way."

"Tell me about it," Cass said. "I've learned that secrets have a way of jumping up and biting you on the butt. We'll probably tell them tomorrow. Maybe casually over lunch. Mom is less likely to blow a fuse if we're in a public place."

"Does this mean you're not having lunch with me?"

"Sorry. We have a lot to take care of tomorrow. Business. We're reopening on Monday. But if you're not busy on Sunday afternoon, I have an idea of a fun thing to do."

"Does it involve a lot of family?"

"Nope. Let's let it be a surprise."

"Give me a hint," he said.

"Do you like bats?"

"Baseball bats?"

"Nope. The critters."

"Like Count Dracula?"

"Not vampire bloodsuckers. The little insect-eating kind, and I'm not telling you any more."

"Come on. Now I'm intrigued."

"Good. I like being a woman of mystery."

When they pulled up to the hotel valet, Cass exited with her big purse, which she'd stowed in the backseat.

"That's the biggest purse I've ever seen you carry," Griff said as he held open the glass door.

"It's the longest one I have that doesn't look like an overnight bag. I have my jogging gear in here."

"Ahh. You planned ahead."

She winked. "I was a Girl Scout."

He laughed. "You make me laugh more than any woman I've ever known. I love that about you."

Her heart gave a little flutter, but she ignored it. She wasn't out for any serious declarations of any shape or form. Griff was fun. Here today, gone tomorrow. Or next week. Or the next.

In the elevator they could barely keep their hands off each

other, and once they were in his room, they didn't even try. The chemistry between them was explosive.

They left a trail of clothes to the bedroom, and by the time they fell in bed together, the only things left were Cass's earrings and Griff's left sock.

"Oh, woman, you set me on fire," Griff said as he stroked her breast.

"The feeling's mutual," she murmured against his lips.

Their joining was quick and hot, interrupted only long enough for protection.

"I'm sorry," Griff said a few moments later. He rested his forehead against hers. "I meant for that to last. I usually have better control."

"Do this a lot, do you?"

"Not as much as you might think. I don't have much time for dating. My mind is generally on work."

"Uh-huh. Sure. And I have this bridge for sale…"

He chuckled and rolled her over on top of him. "Come here, you."

He made love to her again. Slowly. Sweetly. Thoroughly.

Sometime later, they showered, wrapped up in soft hotel robes and fed each other dessert.

"Ahh," she said, licking her lips. "Pecans, caramel and chocolate all in one. What could be better?"

Flicking a little drip off her chin with his tongue, he said, "Give me a few minutes, sweetheart, and I'll show you."

GRIFF COULDN'T SLEEP. He lay holding Cass, listening to her breathing and trying to figure out when his feelings for her had changed. He'd always been satisfied to be a love 'em and leave 'em type. Early on he'd learned commitments could be messy, but none of the women in his past had been like Cass.

He'd never cared for them in the way he was beginning to care for her. Maybe it was because he was getting older. Maybe it was because there was something special about her—her laugh, her fierce dedication to her beliefs, the softness of her skin, the way she touched his heart and warmed him inside. He didn't want to leave her.

Nor did he want to hurt her.

If she knew why he was in Austin and why he'd schemed to meet her that day on the jogging trail, she would be furious. She would never forgive him if she found out. Secrets had a way of jumping up and biting you in the butt, she'd said. He would have to make sure she didn't discover his. He couldn't bear to see her hurt, and he wasn't ready to give her up. He might never be ready.

Hell, he'd already amassed enough money to last most people the rest of their lives. Why did he need more? This deal didn't seem so important any longer.

CASS HAD SLEPT LATER than she intended, and Griff was still out like a light, sleeping so peacefully she hated to awaken him. So she dressed in her jogging clothes and left him a note. She left her other clothes and big purse behind, taking only a few essentials in her fanny pack, and tiptoed out. She'd meant to jog home, but it was getting late, so she grabbed a taxi and climbed out a block from her destination in case her mom and aunt got there early.

They had. Dressed for work, they were just getting out of their car when she trotted up.

"Good morning," Gloria said. "Have you been out for a run already? You don't even look winded."

"I've been practicing," Cass said. She kissed her mom and Aunt Min on their cheeks. "Why are you here so early?"

"There's lots to do yet, and you girls shouldn't have all the burden," Min said. "Besides, what else do we have to do? Have you had breakfast?"

"Not yet. Come upstairs and I'll make us some coffee."

"No need," Gloria said. "We brought a thermos full, and Sunny's stopping by one of the fast food places on her way here."

"Speak of the devil, here she is," Cass said. She waved to her sister as Sunny pulled into the back lot, and went to help carry bags inside. "You got sausage biscuits, I hope?"

"Naturally."

Once they were inside and the alarm turned off, Gloria led them to a table near the front window, and they distributed food and ate.

Sunny bagged their trash and said, "Since all of the dishes and kitchen items have to be washed, let's get the first loads into the dishwashers, and then we can have our company meeting."

"We're having a company meeting?" Cass asked.

"Yes, I left a message on your cell," Sunny said with a little smirk.

"Oops. I haven't checked my messages." She pulled her phone from her fanny pack. "My battery's down, and I forgot to recharge it. Sorry. What are we discussing?"

"A bunch of stuff," Sunny said. "Let's go load dishes first."

After the dishwashers were running, they gathered again at the table and Sunny handed out summaries of the books for both Chili Witches and their other properties, covering the past six months. Cass was very familiar with the figures because she'd helped Sunny and the accountant prepare them.

The elder sisters looked them over carefully. "Very nice," Min said. "It appears as if you girls are doing well with the business."

Gloria beamed with pride. "I knew everything would be in good hands. I didn't know we were worth so much."

"With the downturn in some of the markets," Cass said, "I think our company is doing exceptionally well. So well, in fact, we've had some offers to expand in new directions."

"As well as some other offers," Sunny said, glancing quickly to Cass, "that we'll get to later."

Cass could see those antennae of her mother's going up again. "I'm intrigued now. What are these mysterious other offers?"

"Well," Sunny said, then cleared her throat. "We've had an offer to buy Chili Witches and the entire property around it."

"Really?" Aunt Min said. "For how much?"

When Cass told them the figure, both her mom's and her aunt's eyebrows went sky-high.

"Holy guacamole!" her mom said.

"That's a fortune!" Aunt Min added.

"But, of course," Cass said, "I wrote and declined their offer."

Gloria and Min looked at each other.

"And," Sunny said, "I received a special delivery recently from the same gentleman. This time he upped the offer by ten percent."

"Oh my!" Min said. "He's persistent."

"He's a bastard!" Cass exclaimed. "Dollars to doughnuts his company plans to tear down the whole block and build an ugly high-rise. No way, Jose! Chili Witches is not for sale."

Gloria and Min looked at each other again.

"Let's move on to those offers to expand you mentioned," Min said.

Sunny handed out more papers. "This company would like to introduce our chili as a frozen food item, first in selected markets, then nationally if it goes well. This is their proposal and marketing plan."

"Have you checked out this company?" Gloria asked.

"I did," Cass said. "They have an excellent reputation and a good track record."

"I'd like to give this some more thought," Min said, "but it looks like a fine idea to me."

"I agree. Anything else?"

"Another company that specializes in the start-up of franchises has approached us about franchising Chili Witches," Cass said.

"You mean like McDonald's or KFC?" her mom said.

Cass smiled. "On not so grand a scale."

"Wouldn't that require a tremendous amount of work?" Aunt Min asked.

"Only at first. This company has developed a model for franchising that streamlines the process considerably. They have a lot of experience. Of course, they take a big cut of the pie, as well."

"I think this franchising idea will take several nights sleep, but it sounds a little scary to me," Gloria said. "What do you girls think?"

"We're still sleeping on it as well," Sunny said.

"Wouldn't marketing a frozen chili be in direct competition with franchises?" Aunt Min asked.

"Actually, no," Cass told them. "The stores, as they call them, would be another marketing outlet. Eat some, take some home for the freezer."

There was a rap on the front window, and Cass looked up to see Belle Outlaw Burrell waving and smiling on the other side of the glass. Cass felt the blood drain from her face, and Sunny looked as if she might bolt out the back door.

Chapter Twelve

Cass hadn't felt such panic since she'd been called into the vice principal's office when she was in the eighth grade. No way could she ignore Belle, but she could try her best to head off any problems. Talk about secrets biting you in the butt.

Jumping to her feet, she pasted on a bright smile, waved to Belle and hurried to the front door. She fumbled with the lock and finally got it open. Throwing her arms wide, she ran outside and wrapped her cousin in a big hug.

"For gosh sakes, don't mention the Outlaw family," Cass whispered in her ear. "We haven't told Mother yet. Follow my lead. I'll explain later." She grabbed her hand and dragged her inside.

"Why are you closed?" Belle asked.

"We had a flood," Cass said. "Look, everybody, it's Belle Burrell. Belle, this is our mother, Gloria O'Connor, and our aunt, Minerva O'Connor. We call her Min. Belle is Sunny's and my dear friend from Wimberley. She owns the newspaper there. Mother and Aunt Min just got in from France a couple of days ago. They rented a house there and have been having a grand time."

"Welcome home," Belle said. "I'm delighted to meet you.

Sunny and Cass speak of you often. I dropped by for a visit and a bowl of chili, only to see the closed sign. Am I interrupting something?"

"Not at all," Sunny said. "We're just finishing up a meeting and starting to wash dishes." Sunny explained the vandalism and the flooding.

"How absolutely terrible," Belle said. "How can I help? I'm not much of a cook, but I can wash dishes."

"The kitchen staff is arriving shortly, and they'll see to the rest of the dishes, but thanks, Belle," Cass said. "We plan to reopen on Monday."

Belle turned on the charm and chatted with Gloria and Min about their trip. When she heard that Gloria was a painter, she said, "My mother-in-law is a painter, quite an excellent one. She has a gallery in Wimberley, The Firefly. You must come down sometime and visit. Do you paint, too, Min?"

"Oh, heavens no. I do needlework."

"Don't be modest, Aunt Min," Sunny said. "Her needlework is exquisite. I'm so envious. I can barely sew on a button."

"It was so delightful meeting you," Belle said to the older women, "but I must be running along. I'm sure you must have a world of things to do before the reopening."

Min cocked her head at Belle. "Have we met before? You look very familiar somehow."

"No, I'm sure we've never met."

"Humph," Gloria said. "I should imagine she looks familiar. Look at her and look at your nieces. They could be sisters."

"That must be it," Min said.

"We've heard that before," Cass said. "Strange, isn't it? Belle, I'll walk you out. I want to ask you something." She hooked her arm through her cousin's and practically dragged her out the door.

Once they were outside, Belle said, "I'm sorry I came at an awkward time. I didn't dream they were back yet."

"Not a problem. I'm sorry the situation was uncomfortable for you. We have to tell them about meeting the whole Outlaw family sooner or later, and your visit has given us the perfect opening. I'm glad they got to meet you."

"I hope it turns out well. Oh, before I forget, Frank and Carrie are coming down next weekend, and Carrie said she wants to meet privately with you and Sunny. We'd love to have you join us in Wimberley on Sunday or, if that's not possible, Carrie can come to Austin. I think she wanted to combine everything in one trip if possible."

Curious about the odd request, Cass frowned. Carrie Outlaw, who was married to Frank James Outlaw, judge of the Naconiche County Court of Law, was a former landman for an oil company. She'd come to town to lease drilling rights in the area, and stayed to marry Frank. These days she practiced law in town. "I wonder what she wants?"

"She didn't say, and I didn't ask. Are you free?"

"I'll have to check with Sunny. Shall I get back to you or to Carrie?"

"Me first. I can relay your message, and she can call you if she needs to."

They said goodbye and Cass reentered the dining room. The business with Carrie was intriguing but totally overshadowed by having to deal with telling her mother about their new relationship with the Outlaw family.

Everybody appeared as if they'd been zapped into suspended animation while she was gone. Sunny was sitting stock-still, staring down at her hands; their mom was staring at Sunny; Aunt Min was staring at Gloria.

"Sorry about the interruption," Cass said. "Anything else we need to go over, Sunny?"

"Uh, no. I think we've just about covered everything."

Cass sat back down in the chair she'd vacated earlier and tried desperately to think of the right opening. Her scalp prickled and she began to reexperience the sausage biscuit she'd eaten earlier.

"She's a lovely young woman," Gloria said.

"Who?"

"Belle. What did you say her last name was?"

"Burrell. Her husband's name is Gabe."

"I see," Gloria said, pinning Cass with a sharp gaze, the same gaze that never missed anything. "And what is her father's name?"

"Wes." Cass swallowed. "Wes Outlaw."

One could have heard the proverbial pin drop.

"My stars and garters!" Aunt Min said.

Gloria took a deep breath. "I see. No wonder her resemblance to you is amazing."

"Belle is Belle Starr Outlaw Burrell. We've met the whole family. We didn't go looking for them. One of Belle's brothers came in for lunch one day and, quite by accident we discovered we were cousins. And, Mom, all the Outlaws were delighted to learn about us."

"They've welcomed us into the family with open arms," Sunny said. "They're such nice people, and they're eager to meet you, Mom."

"I see."

"Gloria," Min said quietly, "it was bound to happen sooner or later. Isn't it wonderful things have turned out so well?"

"Of course. I just need a little time to get used to the idea. Now, girls, if you'll excuse us for a while, Min and I have some shopping to do." She rose and walked toward the back exit.

Aunt Min shrugged and whispered, "Don't fret. She'll come around. Just give her a bit of time to chew on it." She patted her nieces' hands, rose and followed her sister.

"That went well," Sunny said, rolling her eyes.

"Actually, it went better than I expected. At least Mom didn't go into hysterics."

"And when," Sunny asked, "did you ever see Mom go into hysterics?"

"Never, now that I think about it. I suppose the closest was when I got a C in conduct in the second grade. Or when you fell off your bike and were all bloody."

"I just hope she isn't too hurt by this," Sunny said.

The kitchen crew arrived just then and the two of them went to get things organized.

They got busy, and Cass didn't remember until later to tell Sunny about Carrie Outlaw wanting to meet with them. Both were curious about the request, but they decided there was no need to speculate until they talked with her. In consideration of their mother, they also decided not to go to Wimberley and spend the day with part of the Outlaw clan just yet.

Cass talked with Carrie that evening, and they agreed to meet for a late Sunday breakfast in Drippings Springs, the small town about halfway between Austin and Wimberley. Even through she tried her best to get more information, Carrie was evasive.

"It's business, and better if we talk in person," Carrie said. "See you in a week."

"Okay." Frustrated and totally baffled, Cass ended the call.

Her cell rang again almost immediately. She recognized the number. Griff.

"Hi," he said. "I've been missing you. Tired?"

"Absolutely pooped. If I had a tub, I'd sit here and soak my feet."

"I have a tub," he said. "And a big swimming pool."

"You know, a swim right now would be fantastic."

"Come on over."

"I can't stay long."

She could practically hear that sexy smile of his over the phone. "I'll take what I can get. Your bathing suit is ready and waiting for you."

THE NIGHT WAS COOL, the water was warm and Griff's kiss was hot.

"Don't get that started," Cass said, pulling away. "I need to get home early."

"I can come home with you."

"I don't think so. My mother's had enough shocks for one day."

"And what was so shocking to her today?" he asked as he lazily sidestroked beside her.

"Belle dropped by."

"Uh-oh."

"Exactly. Sunny and I had to spill the whole thing about meeting the Outlaws."

"Did she explode?"

"No. Strangely enough, after she had time to digest the idea, she took it rather well. I think she was relieved her worst fears hadn't come to pass, that our father's family wasn't horrified to learn of our existence. Still, she's been subdued today."

"At least you don't have the worry hanging over your head." He captured her in his arms again, kissed her again and they sank beneath the water.

She came up sputtering and laughing and splashing him. "Are you trying to drown me? It won't work, you know. At least half the people on this side of the hotel are watching your moves."

"Then come upstairs with me. We'll order a bottle of wine, and I'll massage your feet."

She flipped on her back and floated. "You'd really massage my feet?"

"Of course. You have lovely feet." He stroked her arch and flexed her foot. "I'll even nibble your toes—and anywhere else you name."

His suggestive tone sent shivers over her, and she felt her resolve to leave early quickly fading away. She wasn't nearly as tired as she'd been earlier.

BEFORE THEY GOT TO THE foot massage, Cass and Griff showered, and the shower took much longer and was more intimate than she'd intended. After they'd changed into shorts, Griff took a towel and led her to the sofa.

"Lie down," he said.

She cocked an eyebrow. "What did you have in mind?"

"I promised you a foot massage."

"Yes you did. I thought it had slipped your mind. What are you going to use?"

"My hands. I'm very good with my hands."

Cass chuckled. "I'll grant you that, but I meant do you have lotion or oil?"

Griff looked pained. "I'll run down to the gift shop and get something."

"No need," Cass said. "There should be some lotion in one of those little bottles in the bathroom."

"Right. Be right back."

He was back with a handful of bottles before she got settled. He spread the towel over his thighs, then patted it. "Put your feet up here." After he unscrewed a bottle cap, he sniffed the contents. "This ought to do it."

He picked up her left foot, kissed her big toe, then poured about half the contents on the top of her foot and began to massage.

Griff had been right. He did have wonderful hands. Still, something didn't seem quite right. Cass lifted her head and looked at her foot. Despite his enthusiastic rubbing, the lotion hadn't dispersed at all. True, he'd used quite a bit, but none of it was being absorbed into her skin.

"What did you put on my foot?"

He grinned. "Good-smelling stuff. Like it?"

"Griff, my foot is beginning to lather."

He frowned, then picked up the small bottle he'd used and squinted at the writing on it. Handing it to her, he said, "What does that say?"

She read it and started laughing. "Didn't you read it?"

"I don't have my contacts in."

"I didn't know you wore contacts."

"I do. Otherwise I'm blind as one of those bats you've been talking about. What does it say?"

"Shampoo." She howled with laughter.

Griff wasn't amused. She could tell by the air he turned blue. "I'm sorry. Now I feel like a damned fool."

"I think it's a hoot. It's reassuring to know you're not perfect."

"Honey, trust me, I'm a long way from perfect."

She put her arms around his neck and drew him close. "Couldn't prove it by me."

Chapter Thirteen

It was after midnight before Cass finally made it home and fell into bed. Knowing there were still dozens of last minute things to do the next day, she postponed her Sunday surprise activity with Griff until Monday. He didn't seem to mind. In fact he showed up at Chili Witches Sunday morning with huge boxes of breakfast tacos and doughnuts for everybody.

"Wasn't it sweet of Griff to bring these?" Cass said to her mother as she offered her a taco.

"Very nice of him." Gloria gave Griff a polite smile.

Ben McKee and his brother-in-law, Rick, came in a pickup to return the stored office furniture to its place. Griff pitched in and helped tote the desk, file cabinets and other items to the café's office. With everybody helping, the office was restored quickly and the computer and other electronic equipment plugged up and ready to go.

By one o'clock, the dishes sparkled, the pantry was stocked, the cooler was full and everything was prepared for Monday. The kitchen staff left, Gloria and Min went home for a nap, Rick took off in the pickup and Ben rode home with Sunny. Griff and Cass were left alone to lock up.

"Want to come upstairs and watch the game?" she asked.

"Which game?"

"Whichever one is on. Sunday afternoon is sports or old movies."

"Sure, but I have to get something from the car first. I brought you a present."

"A present. What?"

"It's a surprise." He trotted to his rental car and took out a red gift bag.

When he handed it to her, Cass peeked inside, then smiled. "Massage lotion. There must be a quart here."

"Be Prepared is my motto. Let's go upstairs and I'll massage your tootsies properly." He gave her a devilish grin.

The foot massage didn't happen. They ended up on Cass's sectional watching the Yankees, with Griff's head in her lap. In about twenty seconds flat, he was sound asleep.

When it became apparent he was down for the count, she gently retrieved the remote clutched in his hand and switched to an old musical comedy.

When Cass awoke sometime later, she was surprised to find herself with her head against Griff's shoulder and the Yankees in the last of the ninth.

"I didn't mean to fall asleep," she said, stretching.

"You were tired. I hate to see you work so hard, and it seems as if your talents are wasted running a café. Have you considered doing something else?"

"Well, I've considered running for city council."

"Sounds like a great idea. Do it."

Cass sighed. "Even a campaign would take a tremendous amount of time, and if I got elected, I'd hate to dump most of the responsibility for the business on Sunny. I just couldn't do that to her, especially now when she and Ben are getting married, and she'll have a family to think about."

"Have you ever considered selling the business?" Griff asked.

"Bite your tongue, buster. Sunny and I grew up in Chili Witches, and Mom and Aunt Min worked too hard growing this business to ever sell it. When their folks died, the two of them sold the family farm and put everything they had into buying this property and starting the café. They started small and worked like dogs to get it off the ground. For years they plowed the majority of their profits back into the business. Sunny and I owe it to them to keep it going. It's wonderful that now they can retire and enjoy traveling six months of the year. They're going to Ireland next. Isn't that wonderful?"

"You're a good daughter." He kissed her forehead.

"I try."

"Seems to me this property, being in such a prime location, should be worth a great deal. I would anticipate you could sell it, invest the proceeds properly and have a higher income for your family than you realize now. And without all the work."

Cass felt herself stiffen. "Money isn't the only issue here. A sense of history is just as important. Maybe more so. Why, even our bar is an antique, well over a hundred years old."

Griff flashed his dimples. "Yeah, I remember. From the bawdy house, right?"

"That's right. And a very *famous* bawdy house to boot. It's even mentioned in some of the historical society's publications. I've been thinking about getting a plaque."

"Fine idea."

"Glad you think so. Now, the subject of selling Chili Witches is closed. If you're going to watch another ball game, I'm going to have to have fortification. Want to order a pizza?"

"Sure," he said. "Tell me you don't like anchovies."

"I don't like anchovies. They're like eating salty eyelashes.

No, I take that back. The only way I can tolerate anchovies is in Caesar salad dressing or other stuff where they're mashed up and disguised. And actually, I prefer my Caesar salad without anchovies if given the choice. Did you know that anchovies weren't part of the original recipe?"

"On pizza?"

"In Caesar salad."

"No, I didn't. Should I take notes?"

She laughed and hit him with a pillow. "I'll order the works, no anchovies. Do you want onions?"

"Are you having onions?"

"Sure."

"Then I'll have some, too."

After she phoned in the order, Cass picked up the TV listings to scan, and Griff rested his chin on her shoulder to read. "There's a Dodgers game starting in a few minutes."

"My father would disown me if I watched it. He still hasn't forgiven the Dodgers for moving from Brooklyn to California. Why don't we watch a movie?"

She glanced over the film listings. "Oh, look. *Ghost.* I loved that movie. Whoopi Goldberg won an Oscar for her part. She was hilarious. Have you ever seen it?"

"Not that I recall. What's it about?"

"It's about a ghost. You'll see."

The timing was perfect. The pizza arrived just before the movie started, and they curled up to watch. Cass got teary-eyed at the tender parts and laughed at the funny parts the way she always did. Griff seemed to enjoy it—or at least he didn't complain or groan at inappropriate times the way some men were prone to do.

When it was over, she sniffed, and Griff frowned. "Are you crying?"

"Just a little. I adore that movie."

"It was okay. I suppose I'm more into realism."

"I take it you don't believe in ghosts?" she said.

"I've never seen one. Have you?"

She hesitated. Should she tell him? Griff would think she was nuts. "My sister has," she said as a compromise. It was safer talking about Sunny's experiences than her own.

"Really?" He appeared surprised. "Sunny sees ghosts?"

"Not ghosts. One ghost she's seen several times. She claims she even talks to the Senator—our father, but she calls him the Senator."

"Hmm. What does he look like?"

"Tall, gray-haired, a lot like Uncle Wes."

"How old was he when he died?" Griff asked.

"Forty."

"Was his hair gray then?"

"No. The pictures I've seen of him show his hair was about like mine. Dark."

"Then why would it be gray now? I wouldn't think ghosts would age."

"Huh! I never thought about that. I'll ask Sunny. Please don't mention to her that we discussed this. I'm sure she would be embarrassed. I don't think my mother even knows about it, and I shouldn't have told you."

He picked up Cass's hand and kissed it. "I won't mention it. Thanks for sharing the secret with me."

"Now it's your turn." She cuddled up against him, laying her head on his shoulder and her hand on his chest. "You have to tell me one of your secrets."

She could swear his heart speeded up a tad. Hmm. Had she hit a nerve?

"Must I?"

"That's the way the game is played."

"I stole five dollars from my mother's purse when I was about six. She never knew."

"Why?"

"I wanted to buy a baseball card from Joey Hedgecroft in my first grade class. But I felt so guilty, I couldn't, so I hid the money in my room. Taped it to the underside of a drawer. I think I must have gotten the idea from a TV show."

Cass chuckled. "Is it still there?"

"Nope. I forgot about it, but I found it years later and sneaked the money back into my mother's purse."

"I swiped a nickel once. Someone had left a pile of change on a table in the café. I took a nickel to put in the gum ball machine. My mother caught me, and I tried to lie my way out of it. That made her even more furious, and she made me spit out the gum and wash dishes to earn enough to repay the waiter his nickel. That was the end of my thieving days. I almost died from humiliation. Sunny cried for me."

"And you were how old?" Griff asked.

"About four I think. It was a good lesson. I suspect the incident helped shape the huge value I place on honesty. I think Sunny learned the same thing by observing my experience."

"Crime does not pay."

"You got it. I have no respect for sneaks and liars."

"And lawyers."

She grinned. "In most cases they're the same thing. Present company excluded, of course."

MAYBE IT WAS THE onions on her breath that did it, but Griff soon left, with only a brief kiss at the door. Odd. Very odd. The man was a sex machine. Maybe she shouldn't have told him about Sunny and the ghost. Now he probably thought the family was weird. He likely would have croaked if he knew Cass had seen the Senator, too.

She called Sunny. "Are you alone?"

"Yes," her twin said. "Ben and Jay left earlier. What's up?"

"I have a question about the Senator. Didn't you say his hair was gray?"

"Yes."

"Sunny, when he died, his hair was dark brown, not gray. Why would it be gray now?"

"Hmm. Let me think about it." After a moment, Sunny said, "You know, it seems his hair was darker when I first saw him. It's grayed over the years, as it would have naturally."

"Doesn't it strike you as odd that a ghost ages? How can that be?"

"I don't know," Sunny replied. "Why don't you ask him?"

Chapter Fourteen

Cass sat down at her computer, clicked on Google and typed in "ghosts." She quickly scanned the first couple of pages and even went to several Web sites to check them out, but she found nothing helpful. Most of the stuff was about ectoplasm and orbs and mists and photographs that looked more like anomalies of lighting than ghostly presences. She tried "ghost hair" and found the listings even less helpful. Surely there was somebody around who knew about ghosts—real ghosts, not amorphous blobs.

Well, she'd always been one to rely on primary sources, so she turned off her laptop and stood up.

"Senator?" she whispered.

Nothing.

She walked to the front door, where she'd last seen him. "Senator?"

Still nothing.

Cass walked to her back bedroom and yelled, "Dammit, Senator, where are you when I need to talk to you?"

Nada.

She felt like a total idiot. So much for her ghost hunting exploits. She hadn't actually seen a ghost, she told herself.

Such things didn't exist. Most of the people she'd read about on the Net sounded like nut jobs, didn't they?

Her experiences had a perfectly rational explanation. She'd had some sort of brain blip and imagined the whole thing—like a mirage. A mirage—that was it, especially for Sunny. Her sister had always yearned for a father for as long as Cass could remember. For some reason, Cass didn't miss having a dad as much as her twin did. Sunny's desperate need for a father had conjured one up—like a thirsty man lost in the desert conjures up an oasis or a lonely child creates an imaginary friend.

Forget it, Cass told herself. Why had she become obsessed about an imaginary man and his imaginary hair? Who cared?

She had a stack of reading she needed to do for POAC. With all the chaos, she'd let her duties in the organization slide this week. After she dressed for bed, she plumped up three pillows against her headboard, climbed between the sheets and started reading the material Karen, POAC's secretary, had dropped off yesterday. Cass had to be ready for a meeting with the board tomorrow morning.

CASS AWOKE WITH a start. Her glass-block window showed it was still dark outside, and she glanced at her digital clock. The red numerals read 4:18. A dream had awakened her. A very odd dream.

She lay in bed, unmoving, and mulled over the contents. They'd been walking through a rose garden, she and the Senator, strolling along and enjoying the beauty and fragrance of the flowers.

"I heard you calling," he'd said.

"Why didn't you answer?"

"I didn't want to frighten you. And, too, I wasn't truly sure you wanted me to answer."

"I suspect you're right." She laughed at herself. "I'm not frightened of you now. I had a question to ask you."

He smiled. "About my hair."

"Yes."

"Appearances don't matter very much. What's inside is what counts. Wherever I am, however I look, I'm your father, and I love you very much. Had you rather see me this way?" His appearance suddenly changed from a distinguished older man with gray hair to a much younger man with dark hair who favored Sam Outlaw a great deal.

She gasped at the sudden and startling transformation.

"Or this way?" He turned back into the gray-haired man. "Which one seems like your father?"

"The later, of course. I understand," she said. "You've aged along with us for our sakes. Which are you really?"

"I'm both. And neither. But I'm always around when you and Sunny call. At least for now." In the dream he'd broken off a rose and put it in Cass's hair. "It's important for you to always remember to follow your heart. Don't forget that."

Now, in her bedroom, she could still smell the sweet scent of the rose, but when she reached for it in her hair, it wasn't there.

Tears filled her eyes. "Oh, Daddy," she whispered into the dark.

AT TEN O'CLOCK, CASS called the meeting to order. Five members of the board, Karen and herself were present. Gordon Velt, a sociology professor at UT and vice president of the board, was out of town. The others were Anita Rojas, a real estate agent; Herman Jacobs, an arborist; Martin Sevier, publisher of a weekly newspaper; and Louella Johnson, a retired school librarian who served as treasurer. Several other members of their organization served in advisory positions and headed various committees, but weren't in attendance.

After getting through their usual agenda, including learning from Louella about a treasury that needed a few more healthy donations, Anita, the real estate agent, brought something to their attention. "Scuttlebutt has it that a representative of outside interests is in town checking out several commercial sites suitable for a new high-rise."

Herman and Martin groaned. "Just what we need," Herman said. "Do you know which sites?"

"Those I know about—one on West Ninth and one on Guadalupe—probably aren't of specific interest to us," Anita said. "I don't know what other properties might be involved through direct negotiations with owners."

"Do you know who the party is or what company he or she represents?" Cass asked.

Anita shook her head. "Sorry. The agent involved is keeping the information close to his vest. I'll stay alert and see if I can find out. As soon as I know anything, I'll let you know."

"Do that," Cass said. "And I'll get Darlene's development committee busy beating the bushes for funds for the coffer in case we have a fight on our hands."

"Which we will," Martin said, "sooner or later."

"We've had another offer to buy the Chili Witches property," Cass told them. "I wonder if it's the same firm as the person in town scouting out sites."

"You're not going to sell, are you?" Martin asked.

"When pigs fly," Cass said. "Any other business?"

They discussed three other minor concerns, then ended the meeting.

Anita stopped Cass on their way out. "Are you interested

in selling either this property or the one next door? I have a client who may be interested in one or both houses."

"I don't think so. I plan to live here and rent out the other one. Things have been pretty hectic lately, and I haven't been able to meet with the contractor to start renovations. Hopefully, I can get on it soon and be ready to move in by the end of summer."

"I heard about the flood at Chili Witches," Martin said. "Is everything okay now?"

"Yes, we're reopening today."

"I understand it was malicious mischief. Do the police have any suspects?"

"Not that we've heard," Cass said.

"You mean it was deliberate?" Anita asked.

Cass nodded.

"Do you think it has anything to do with your being president of POAC?"

"I hope not, but I have no way of knowing."

"That's terrible," Anita said. "Just terrible. I'm incensed about someone doing something so needlessly destructive. Was your lovely bar damaged?"

"Luckily, no. The floors in the dining room got the worst of it, and they've been replaced."

"I'll stop by for lunch one day this week and check them out," Martin said.

Cass waved goodbye to the departing board and stayed behind a few minutes to go over a few things with Karen. Since it was nearing lunchtime, they walked to Katz's Deli for a Reuben.

WHEN CASS ARRIVED HOME an hour later, she was surprised at the number of cars still in the lot and on the street. Going in the back way of Chili Witches, she ran into a frazzled Aunt Min in jeans and a red tee.

"What are you doing here?" Cass asked.

"Your mother and I came to help. Good thing we did. It's been a mob scene here. I think every cop in Austin has been in. We're doing a bang-up business. A few more days like this will make up for the losses of last week."

"That's great. Need more help?"

"Ask Sunny, but I think it has slowed to manageable now."

Cass found her sister, who told her everything was under control and to enjoy the rest of her day off. Since Cass was picking up Griff soon, she didn't argue.

If he was still interested in their excursion. After his odd behavior last night, she wasn't sure. He hadn't called to cancel, so she assumed it was still on. She'd made reservations for a Segway tour of the city, ending at the Ann Richards Bridge on Congress. The bridge, renamed after the late governor, joined the two halves of Austin separated by the Colorado River and its reservoir, Lady Bird Lake. She'd seen the Segway riders around town, and she'd been eager to learn to ride one. Or drive one. Or whatever. It looked like fun. She hoped Griff thought so.

At the appointed time, she drove to his hotel and was pleased to find him waiting outside for her and dressed in the jeans she'd suggested he wear.

"Hey, babe," Griff said as he climbed into her car.

"Hey, yourself. Ready for an adventure?"

"Always. Where are we going?"

"Not far. In fact, just a few blocks from here." She headed out to the place where she'd been directed. "First, we have to have a training session."

"A training session? Are we going skydiving?"

"Lord, no. You won't see me jumping out of a plane. Have you ever done it?"

"Nope," he said, "but I've always wanted to try."

"Must not have wanted to too badly," she said, "or you'd have done it."

Griff laughed. "Point taken."

She soon pulled into the lot where the tour started and the training session was held.

"Segways!" he said.

"Yep. Ever been on one?"

"Never, but I've always—"

"Wanted to try," she finished for him. "Me, too. Want to give it a whirl? They'll guide us on a tour of interesting places in downtown Austin, and we'll end up watching the bats."

"I'm game. Let's go." He put his arm around her waist as they walked up to the training area. "Thanks for thinking of this."

Learning to ride one of the two-wheeled contraptions, which reminded Cass a little of a cross between an old-fashioned push lawn mower and the front end of a scooter, wasn't as difficult as she'd thought. You just stood on the platform between the wheels and leaned in the direction you wanted to go, then moved upright to stop—an intuitive connection between rider and machine. It had fat tires and all sorts of internal gyroscopes and high tech stuff. If you wanted to turn right or left, you simply pulled the handlebars in the corresponding direction. Easy. And fun.

Soon she, Griff and the other tourists were zipping around the practice course like pros and having a blast. They had an excellent guide, well versed in Austin history, who led them on the city tour, with stops at the state capitol and the historic Driskill Hotel, as well as some of the monuments and statues and notable houses around town. They rode down the length of Sixth Street and through the Second Street shopping district, and tootled around the lake. The tour was a lengthy one, and they ended up on the banks near the bridge at dusk.

As the lights of the city came on and the sun sank beneath the horizon, they dismounted and hung their helmets on the handlebars to see the final act of the show. Their guide stayed to watch their machines, and most of their group walked up onto the pedestrian walkway of the wide bridge. Cass and Griff lagged behind.

"Have you enjoyed this?" she asked.

He put his arm around her waist and kissed her nose. "I've had a fantastic time. Makes me feel like a kid again. Thanks for thinking of it. Is this where we see the bats?"

"Yep," she said. "They should be leaving at any time."

"Are you sure they won't suck our blood?"

Cass poked him in the side. "Positive."

Griff looked around. "I can't believe so many people showed up to watch bats fly out from under a bridge."

"Just wait, Mr. Smarty-pants."

"Smarty-pants?" He laughed. "I don't believe anybody's ever called me smarty-pants before."

"Sorry," Cass said. "Holdover from childhood. Look!" She pointed to where a few bats were beginning to take flight.

"Is that it?"

"No, that's just the beginning. Let's go watch from the bridge."

They hurried to the railing and watched the sky fill with tiny animals fluttering from beneath the bridge and turning into black, winding streams against the faint pinks and grays of the gathering dusk. As wave after wave took flight, people around them began to ooh and aah and applaud.

"Good Lord!" Griff said. "I've never seen anything like it. There must be thousands of them."

"Told you. There are about a million and a half at last estimate."

"Are they here all the time?" Griff asked, keeping his eyes on the spectacle.

"Nope. Only from about March through October. Just like birds, they head south for the winter."

They seemed to go on in never-ending streams for a half hour or more, and when the last bat had left in the growing darkness, Cass and Griff rode with the group back to the assembly area and to Cass's car.

"Want to have dinner?" he asked.

"Sure. How about some Mexican food at Chuy's? Since I'm working tomorrow, I need to make it an early evening."

"Not too early, I hope," Griff said. "I'm leaving for New York tomorrow."

Chapter Fifteen

The bottom dropped out of Cass's stomach. Griff was leaving? Already? Well, it wasn't as if she didn't expect him to leave sooner or later, but she'd ignored the reality. She tried to wrap her mind around it, but it wouldn't wrap.

Damn! She hadn't thought this would hit her so hard or hurt so badly. She wanted to cry, but refused to let a single tear escape. That's what she deserved for getting too deeply involved. No way would she let him know how his leaving affected her.

Swallowing back her emotions and trying for a casual tone, she said, "Business here finished?"

"Not on your life. I'll be back in a few days. Just some things I need to tend to in New York. Will you miss me?"

"Of course. Will *you* miss *me?*"

"Cass, I miss you every minute we're not together," he said softly. "I'd rather stay in Austin, but this trip can't be avoided."

Her heart gave a little flutter. She hoped he meant it. She really hoped he meant it, because she felt the same way. Was she falling in love with another New York lawyer? Surely not.

Later, as they sat in Chuy's, sipping on frozen margaritas, Cass said, "I'd like to ask you something, if you don't mind."

"Ask anything you'd like."

"Why did you leave so abruptly last night? Was it the talk about ghosts?"

He chuckled. "The talk about ghosts? No, of course not. I left because I knew you were tired, and I forced myself to leave before I stayed and kept you up all night." He reached for her hand and stroked the back of it with his thumb. Those incredible blue eyes captured hers. "Cass, somehow you've wrapped yourself around my heart. I can't seem to get enough of you, and you're on my mind all the time. Why do you think that is?"

For a moment she could only stare at him while ripples of tenderness and longing rose up in her like champagne bubbles. "I—I don't know."

"I think I'm falling for you."

She swallowed. "You do?"

"I do. And I'm hoping you're feeling something special for me, too."

"I do. I mean, I like you very much, Griff. Too much, perhaps."

"Too much? How can that be?"

"My last serious relationship left some deep scars. I'm still a little gun-shy."

"The lawyer?" he asked. "The one from New York who soured you on the profession?"

She wasn't at all surprised Griff had surmised correctly that she'd had a bad relationship with a lawyer. He was very perceptive. "Yes, but he wasn't the only reason I soured on the profession. Although I'll admit he was representative of everything I abhorred about my situation. He stole my ideas and presented them to the senior partners as his own, and got a big leg up by doing so. Worse, he didn't see anything wrong with his dirty dealing. Fed me some line of crap about it not mattering whose ideas they were as long as they solved a problem the firm was having. Yay, team. Rah, rah, rah. Bull patties!

"He knocked me down and stomped all over my back to make points with the partners. I couldn't do anything about it without sounding like a whining woman."

"The bastard!"

"Uh, no. Literally, *I'm* a bastard. He's a dickhead." Griff grinned. "Or worse."

"Daniel was an egotistical, manipulating liar who used me for his own purposes." She found her hand balled into a fist and shaking. "See, it still enrages me to talk about it. I can't believe I didn't get his number sooner. Not only did I feel betrayed, I felt like a gullible fool."

"Cass, I'm not Daniel," Griff said quietly.

"I know."

"I could break his knees for hurting you. Want me to take my baseball bat and look him up when I'm in Manhattan?"

She smiled. "I'm tempted to say yes. But, no."

"How about we get our food packed in take-out boxes?"

"Excellent idea. And a paper cup for our margaritas."

AS SHE LAY WRAPPED in Griff's arms, savoring the warm afterglow of their lovemaking, Cass would have been content to stay there forever. Not only was he a fabulous lover, Griff was everything else a woman would want. He was handsome, charming and considerate. He was thoughtful and kind and fun. He was every woman's dream. Surely she was missing something. Nobody could be that perfect.

Or was he one of a kind and she simply the luckiest woman in Texas for running into Griffin Mitchell on the jogging trail?

He nuzzled her forehead. "What are you thinking?"

"Truthfully? I was thinking that you're too good to be true. I'm wondering what's the fatal flaw in this mix."

"I'm not that good, but I'll try my best to be good enough for you. The luckiest day of my life was when I met you. My mom is going to love you."

Her cell phone rang. She located her bag and checked the ID. "Speaking of moms…" She sighed and answered.

"Cass, where are you, dear?"

"I'm out with Griff."

"I see." Her tone was decidedly stiff. "Well, I won't keep you. I just wanted to let you know Min and I will be there about eleven-thirty to help with the rush hour in case things are as busy as they were today."

"Thanks, Mom. I appreciate that."

"No bother. We're happy to help. Don't stay out too late. You need your rest."

"I won't, Mom. Good night."

"Gloria, I presume?" Griff asked when she'd closed the phone.

Cass nodded. "She and Min are coming in to help with the noon rush. We had wall-to-wall people today. Maybe things will ease off a little tomorrow. I need to go home and get a good night's sleep." She kissed his chin and poked a finger in his dimple. "For some reason I don't sleep much when you're around."

"My scintillating personality?"

"That, too."

Cass started to rise, but Griff pulled her back into his arms. "I don't want you to leave." His tongue slowly traced the outline of her lips, and his hand slid up her leg. "Ever."

One kiss and she melted.

She got home an hour later than she'd planned.

THE PACE WASN'T QUITE as hectic at noon as it had been the day before, but there were no empty tables in Chili Witches, and a few people had to wait five minutes or so.

By one forty-five, things had slowed considerably. Cass, her mother and Aunt Min sat down to have a glass of tea and a salad.

"Business is booming," Min said. "I was just telling your mother that when we first started, we were lucky to have four of our six tables occupied."

Gloria nodded. "Chili Witches has come a long way over the years. I hate to see you girls slave so hard and such long hours. You should have families, travel, have fun, not work yourselves to a frazzle. Why—"

She stopped speaking abruptly and turned pale as she stared at the front door. Cass turned around to see what caused her mother's reaction. Sam Outlaw was hanging his white hat on the rack.

Oh, dear.

Her hand splayed against her chest and her eyes wide, Gloria continued to stare. "You don't have to tell me who he is. It's one of Wes's boys. He's the spitting image of your father."

"It's Sam," Cass said. "Do you want to meet him?"

"I suppose I must."

"Not if it's going to upset you, Mom."

"Well, I want to meet him," Min said. "It's like seeing a ghost."

Cass rose and met Sam as he waited by the bar. "Am I welcome?" he asked. "Is that your mother?"

"It is. Mom and my aunt. If Mom looks a little stunned, it's because she says you're the spitting image of my father."

"That's what I've been told. I barely remember him. I can

go sit in a corner—or leave if it's an awkward time. Have you told her about us yet?"

"Yes, we had to fess up. It's okay. Come join us."

Cass led Sam to the table and introduced him to Gloria and Min.

"Ladies, it's a pleasure to meet you. Belle said you were lovely, and I can see she wasn't exaggerating."

Gloria chuckled. No, she *giggled.* "Oh, go on with you, Sam. I can tell you're an Outlaw for sure."

Sam grinned. "That I am, ma'am, and I'm delighted to meet you. My mama and daddy are having a fit to meet you, too. In fact the whole family is chomping at the bit to get to know you ladies. We're all crazy about Sunny and Cass."

"May I get you something to eat, Sam?" Min asked.

"Why, yes ma'am, thank you. I'd love a bowl of that fine chili and a big glass of iced tea."

Min and Gloria both smiled, and Cass bit the inside of her cheek to keep from laughing out loud. Sam was turning it on full blast.

Gloria asked about the rest of the Outlaw family, and Sam whipped out his wallet and began pulling out pictures, first of his wife, Skye, then of the other families. "And this," he said, "is my oldest brother, Colt, and his wife and little girl."

He had group pictures of everybody, and he proudly displayed them and told a little about each one. Cass wondered if he carried all those photos in his wallet as a rule. It made his billfold very fat.

Sam continued to charm the ladies while he ate his chili and drank his tea, then topped them off with a big bowl of peach cobbler and ice cream. "I *love* this cobbler," he said as he shoveled it in.

"Would you like another?" Min asked.

"Oh, no, ma'am. I gotta keep fit to catch crooks."

"What are you doing in Austin today, Sam?" Cass asked.

"Talking to the sheriff about a cold case we're working." To Gloria and Min he said, "I'm a Texas Ranger based in San Antonio and part of a team that focuses on old cases that were never solved."

Gloria nodded. "I noticed your badge."

"Well, I hate to eat and run," Sam said, "but duty calls."

He pulled out his wallet again, but Gloria waved it away. "Our treat."

"Why, thank you, ma'am. I'm honored." He stood. "I'm looking forward to meeting you again soon."

Cass walked him to the door. "I thought I was going to have to get out the shovel for a minute."

Sam grinned. "Did I do good?"

"You were superb."

He kissed her cheek, grabbed his hat and left.

When Cass returned to the table, Gloria sighed. "Such a nice young man. Wes must be very proud of him. Too bad he's married and your cousin."

"Well, he's not available," Cass said, "and I really like Griff. Don't you?"

"Not particularly," her mother said. "Min, are you ready to go get those geraniums?"

"Wait a minute," Cass said. "Why don't you like Griff?"

"I'm not exactly sure. I think it's something in his eyes."

"But, Mom, his eyes are gorgeous. You said so yourself."

"I'm not talking about their appearance. It's more about— oh, I don't know, maybe the expression. He's a bit too…"

"Slick," Min finished.

Exasperated at the two of them, Cass clenched her teeth.

"You've said that before. If you're talking slick, Sam Outlaw is slicker than goose grease."

"Oh, not like Sam," Gloria said. "He's just a good old Texas boy with a knack for charming bull doo-doo. I'm talking about a different kind of slick. An underhanded kind of slick. Mark my word, Cass, Griffin Mitchell will break your heart."

"That man is just not copacetic," Min said. "Is he married?"

Cass's heart almost stopped, and a strange feeling came over her. "Of course not! Whatever gave you such an idea?"

Married? Surely not. The thought had never occurred to her. If he was married, if he'd been lying to her, she would die. She would just die.

Chapter Sixteen

Griff was *not* married. Cass refused to allow herself to even consider such a possibility. For the rest of the day, when the thought would pop into her head, she immediately quashed it and busied herself with some task or other—which wasn't hard to do. They'd had a bang-up business for dinner as well. Even the food editor at one of the papers stopped by to see how things were going, and promised a mention in her column. Free publicity was always a help, though if business got much better, Cass didn't know where she would put people.

When her cell phone rang at about nine-thirty and she saw who was calling, Cass was conflicted. Part of her was thrilled that Griff was calling; another part of her was distressed. She was going to have to ask.

Walking to her office for privacy, she said, "Hello, Griff. How's the Big Apple?"

"Noisy and fast. I've been spoiled lately. My blood pressure is already up ten points. Or twenty. How was your first day back?"

"Hectic. Scads of customers. Griff?"

"Yes?"

"I have to ask you something."

"Shoot."

"Promise you won't be offended."

"Sounds ominous. I promise."

She hesitated. Gutsy as she ordinarily was, it was a question she didn't want to ask. Maybe she really didn't want to hear the answer—or at least one of the possible answers. Taking a deep breath, she said, "Griff, are you married?"

When he stopped laughing, he said, "Whatever gave you that idea?"

"You didn't answer the question."

"No, babe, I'm not married. Never have been. I've proposed to only one person in my life, and that was Lisa Davenport when we were in the second grade."

"Did she accept?"

"As I recall, she punched me in the stomach and ran away."

"How terrible."

"I thought so. Scarred me for life." He chuckled. "Why did you ask me if I was married?"

"Someone once told me men over thirty-five who aren't married are either gay or rejects. I know you aren't gay, and I can't imagine you being anybody's reject, so that leaves being married."

"Oh, I don't know. Remember Lisa."

Cass could hear the amusement in his voice and felt like an idiot for asking. "You are over thirty-five, aren't you?"

"I am." He rattled off his birthday to verify his age.

"You have a birthday coming up next month."

"I do," he said. "Are you going to bake a cake for me?"

"Probably not, but I know a wonderful bakery that makes fantastic birthday cakes. When are you coming back to Austin?"

"I'm not sure. I have several meetings set up. It might be the weekend before I get back. Will you miss me?"

"Of course I will," Cass said. "I've grown very used to your company."

They soon said good-night, and Cass began her customary closing procedure. Talking with Griff had given her a warm glow, and she smiled as she stashed the day's take in the big office safe. Either she or Sunny would deposit the cash and checks in the bank the next day.

By the time she'd set the alarm and locked up, she was bushed. Twelve- and fourteen-hour days were a bitch. What a treat it would be to fall in bed and sleep late the following morning.

Unfortunately, her sleep was restless, and the contractor called her at seven-thirty the next morning. She agreed to meet him at the POAC office in an hour to discuss renovations. Even though she had to drag herself to the shower, stinging water and excitement about the project soon perked her up, and she hurriedly dressed and drove to the site.

The contractor, Greg Gonzales, was waiting for her, clipboard in hand. She and Sunny and Greg had gone to high school together, and he had an excellent reputation for building and remodeling. He was as handsome as ever. In fact, she'd had a major crush on him when she'd been a sophomore, but he was a senior and interested in dating older girls.

"Hey, Greg," she called, getting out of her car. "I hope I haven't kept you waiting."

He grinned. "Nope. I just got here, and I've been looking at some of the other houses in the neighborhood. Some are looking good, others not so good."

"I know. As I told you, those of us who bought houses on this street are committed to restoring them to either live in, rent or sell. I plan to live in this one and rent the other, and the sooner I can get them renovated, the sooner I'll get a return on my money."

"I did some work on the house across the street a few years ago, and these houses all seem to be basically sound. They have good bones. Mostly they just need some repairs here and there, some updating and a lot of paint. Let's walk through your properties so you can tell me what you want."

They went through POAC headquarters first, discussing the changes she wanted in each room, especially the kitchen and bathrooms. Greg examined every nook and cranny and made copious notes. They did the same for the house next door.

"I think you made a good buy here," Greg said. "With your proximity to downtown, and with the other houses on the street being renovated, your property will be worth double or triple what you paid for it when it's fixed up. I'll get back to you with estimates in a day or two."

"Great, Greg. If we agree on price, when can you start?"

"Right away. My crew is finishing a big job now. Say, I notice the house down at the end of the street is for sale by the owner, and looks like it could use some work as well. Know anything about it?"

"I do. It recently came on the market. A friend of ours bought the house and moved in, planning to renovate a little at a time, but he's been transferred to Pittsburgh. You interested?"

"I might be…if the price was right." He winked. "It might be a good investment—and I could give you a better deal if my crew is working on three houses right here together."

"I'll call you with Oscar's number."

"Don't bother. I can get it off the sign."

"Mention my name," Cass said.

"Count on it."

After Greg left, she wandered around the yard, with its scraggly bushes and weedy lawn, and felt real envy for Sunny's well-kept lawn and garden. Cass could almost imagine a chamois-colored cottage with black shutters, white trim and a red door. The porch and steps would be updated and big pots of geraniums or marigolds would flank the doorway. The lush buffalo grass lawn would set off the flag-stone walkway and native plants would complement the lines of the house.

She smiled and sighed. Her very own place.

What color would she paint the house next door? Maybe a pale yellow or a sage-green. Or dove gray with maroon-and-white trim. It was fun thinking about it, but she didn't want to get too carried away. She had some money left over from the killing she'd made when she sold her Manhattan condo, and she'd saved quite a bit since she'd been home, but she'd have to be careful with costs. She didn't have an endless supply of money to squander, and she didn't want to overdo for the neighborhood.

Still smiling, she headed off to the paint and flooring stores for samples. She'd also need to scout around for appliances and get an idea of what she wanted—and what her budget could stand. Someone had told her there was a fantastic ware-house on Burnet Road with great deals on close-out items and stuff with tiny scratches or dents not even noticeable. And she had to think about cabinet styles and hardware and light fixtures and a thousand other details.

Her days off were going to be plenty busy. Maybe it was a good thing Griff would be in New York for the next little while.

Or not.

WHEN CASS STOPPED BY Chili Witches midafternoon, Sunny eyed her bulging tote. "What's that?"

"Samples."

"Are you in training for a door-to-door job?"

Cass laughed. "Nope. I'm finally starting on my house. I met with Greg Gonzales this morning for estimates. These are paint samples and floor samples and brochures and catalogs I have to pore over. Do you know how hard it is to choose between daffodil and sunbeam?"

"Colors, I presume? Want a glass of tea?"

"I'd be forever in your debt, sis. Thanks."

Sunny poured two glasses and led Cass to a table.

Cass took a sip of tea. "Ahhh. Perfect. Where are Mom and Aunt Min?"

"I think they were going to a movie with some friends. I told them not to come in tonight. I can manage."

"Want me to go to the bank?"

"Sure, if you don't mind. Do you have a date with Griff tonight?"

"No, he's back in New York."

Sunny looked stunned. "For good?"

"Not according to him. He has a few days business there. Meetings, he said. He plans to be back in Austin by the weekend."

"Don't forget our meeting with Carrie Sunday morning," Sunny said.

"I haven't forgotten. Wonder what she wants?"

"Beats me."

"Guess who came in for a late lunch yesterday?" Cass asked.

"I already know. Sam. Mom told me. I think she and Aunt Min fell in love with him."

Cass took another big swallow of tea. "Did she also tell you how much he looks like our father?"

Sunny shook her head. "She neglected to mention that little fact."

"Hmm. I thought her eyes were going to pop out when she

first spotted him. He already had an advantage before he turned on the charm—and he turned it on full blast. You could have bottled it and sold it for clover honey."

"I think Mom is actually considering meeting other members of the family."

"Fantastic," Cass said.

"I'm not sure she's ready for the whole mob at once, but maybe one of us could take her and Aunt Min down to Wimberley sometime and have lunch with Belle and Flora. Maybe visit Flora's art gallery."

"Good idea. Perhaps we turned down Belle's invitation for Sunday too soon. I think the only ones coming from Naconiche are Frank and Carrie. Want me to call Belle and reinvite ourselves?"

"No. Something tells me to leave it as is."

"Okay by me." Cass drank the last of her tea and stood. "Let's get the bank bag, and I'll be off."

CASS STARED AT THE color swatches taped to her bedroom wall, trying to decide which tones would be best for her living room. To get some ideas, she'd watched several episodes on HGTV. Several of the decorators were painting rooms gray or some shade of purple. She wasn't a fan of either color.

Maybe she should hire a decorator to help her. Trying to make so many decisions made her brain hurt. It was so much easier if you had a yellow wall to begin with and had to find things that would coordinate, rather than decide the color of the wall so you could find things to coordinate with it. She wanted to scream in frustration.

Luckily, she was saved from a meltdown when the phone rang.

"Hey, gorgeous, what are you doing?" Griff asked.

"I'm about to have a screaming hissy fit."

"Sounds serious," he said. "What's up?"

She told him about the houses and her frustration with color chips. "It's running me crazy, and I've barely started."

"Why don't you hire a decorator?"

"I considered it, but not for long. I love decorating."

He was quiet for a moment. "Cass, that doesn't compute."

She chuckled. "My frustration will pass, and once I get some basic selections, everything else will be easy. What's all that noise?"

"I'm at the airport."

Her heart sped up. "Are you on your way back to Austin?"

"I wish," he said. "I'm on my way to Miami. I have some business there I must take care of. I'm not sure how long it will take. Hopefully, only a day or two. It may be the first of the week before I can return to Austin. Cass, I have to go. My flight's being called. I'll try to get back with you tomorrow or Friday for sure. Love you. Bye."

Cass sat there, stunned, listening to dead air.

Chapter Seventeen

The news Griff was flying off to Miami didn't startle her nearly as much as his last words. "Love you," he'd said. Was that a casual farewell or did it mean something more?

And why was she obsessing about it? The *L* word hadn't been mentioned before. *Cool it, Cass,* she told herself. *Don't rush things. Take it slow and easy.* In the first place, she might have misunderstood him.

No, she hadn't misunderstood. She'd heard what she'd heard. Loud and clear. And it wasn't three little words. It was two. Unless you counted "Bye." And she didn't.

Oh, cripes! Forget it. Concentrate on the color chips. Concentrate!

When she'd finally selected colors for the outside of her house, she began to laugh. She'd picked the exact same hues as Sunny's house. Oh, the chamois shade she'd picked might have a tiny bit more gold, but basically they were the same. Would Sunny mind?

She'd have to ask, but knowing her sister, there wouldn't be a problem. No wonder Cass had immediately loved Sunny's house.

For the other house, she picked a soft gray trimmed with

white, with a yellow front door. People were supposed to be drawn to yellow doors. By the time she went to bed, she'd selected wall colors for the entire interior of both places. All the paint was eco-friendly, and she was putting down bamboo floors everywhere except the kitchens and bathrooms, which would be tile. Greg Gonzales had promised to use reclaimed lumber wherever he could, and to think green in other ways.

Cass was really getting excited to move on the renovations, and she hoped Greg's bid was on target. Two months ago she'd gotten an estimate from another contractor, whose figure had been exorbitant. Several people had recommended Greg, and she had good feelings about the whole venture.

THE FOLLOWING MORNING, Greg called as she was getting dressed. "I have your estimate together," he told her.

"Already? I like the way you work."

"I aim to please. When and where can I drop it off?"

"I'm working today at Chili Witches. I'll be there until closing. Anytime is fine with me."

"Great," Greg said. "By the way, I made a deal with your friend Oscar, and I'm buying his house down the street from yours. It worked out well for both of us. He needed to move to his new job as soon as possible, and I'll soon be starting renovations there as well."

"Fantastic. See you later."

She finished dressing and hurried downstairs to open.

Sometime after eleven, Cass was in the office chasing down an invoice when her mother stuck her head in. "Someone out front is asking for you," Gloria said. Her mouth drew into a sly smile. "A man. A very handsome man."

"Must be Greg Gonzales. He said he'd be dropping by."

"The same Greg Gonzales you went to school with? The football player you used to swoon over when you were fifteen?"

"The very one. You don't forget much, do you, Mom?"

"How could I forget? For a year I never heard such sighing over a boy. It looks like you finally have your chance. He seem very nice."

"Don't go matchmaking, Mom. He's a contractor, here to drop off an estimate for renovating the houses I bought. Besides, I imagine he's married with four kids by now."

"Maybe so, but I didn't see a ring on his finger. I checked."

Cass shook her head. "Rings don't mean anything these days, especially in his business. They're sometimes a safety hazard."

She hurried out to meet Greg, who was standing by the bar with a large envelope in his hand.

He smiled when he saw her. "Good morning, Cass."

"Hi, Greg. That for me?" She motioned to the envelope, which he handed to her. "Have time for me to buy you a cup of coffee?"

"As a matter of fact, I thought I'd grab a hamburger and some fries while I'm here. I've been up since five with my roofing crew, and it's time for my lunch."

"Sure. Where would you like to sit? You've beat most of the lunch crowd. Grab any table you want."

"Do you have time to join me?"

"For a minute. I'm eager to see your figures." She turned to tell her mother to watch the door, and almost fell over her. "Eavesdropping?" she whispered.

"Certainly not," Gloria said. "Go ahead and have a bite with your friend. Min and I can handle everything. After all, we did it for years without any help."

Cass gave her an exasperated eye roll and trailed after Greg.

Gloria followed. Cass had no choice except to introduce her to the contractor.

"I'm so delighted to meet you, Greg. I remember you as a boy. Now, what can I get you two for lunch?"

Greg ordered, and Cass said, "I think I'll just have coffee for now, Mom. Thanks."

She could see her mother open her mouth to argue, but Cass gave a small shake of her head. "Wonderful," Gloria said. "I'll get those drinks right out."

Actually, one of the waiters brought the drinks, and Cass opened the envelope to check the estimates. After a quick scan of the figures, she said, "I'll want to study this in more detail before I give you a final answer, but my first impression is that it looks very satisfactory. When can you start?"

"Anytime you give the word. We should be finished with our current job by the weekend, and I can have a crew there Monday morning. If you want to wait—"

"I don't. I've put this off long enough. I'd like to get started as soon as possible. I'll check your estimates later this afternoon and get back to you. Is this your cell number?" She pointed to the letterhead.

"No. Let me write it down for you." He made a note on the outside of the envelope.

"I'm so excited about this. I already have the paint colors and flooring picked out. I'm going over in the morning to take some measurements so I can begin to plan for rugs and furniture."

"Want me to help with the measurements?" he asked.

"Oh, not necessary, Greg. I'm sure you have better things to do."

"Not at all. My men can work without me for a while, and I'd like to talk to you about a fireplace."

"A fireplace?"

"Yes. I'm thinking about adding a gas fireplace to the house I'm buying from Oscar, and I was wondering if you're interested in one in your house as well."

"I hadn't even thought about it, but that's a wonderful idea. How much would it cost?"

"I'm going to get some figures together later this afternoon," he said, "and I can let you know tomorrow."

The waiter appeared with Greg's hamburger and fries. Aunt Min was right behind him with another tray. Cass again made introductions.

Aunt Min gushed a bit over him, then said, "I'm trying out new recipes for sweet potato empanadas, Cass, and I wish you would try out these two kinds and the different sauces and see what you think." She laid out two plates, one holding baked empanadas, the other fried, along with three sauces, side plates and silverware. "I just finished them."

"Could I do that later? I need to get back to work. We have customers coming in."

"Oh, pish," her aunt said. "Gloria and I can handle everything. Greg, I'd like your opinion as well. After you finish your hamburger, of course." She smiled brightly.

"Yes, ma'am," he said. "I'll give them a try."

After Min wiggled her fingers and left, he asked, "Are your mother and aunt twins, too?"

"No," Cass said. "But they do look a lot alike. And they conspire in tandem."

Greg looked puzzled.

"Never mind." She was glad he hadn't snapped to their obvious efforts to get something going between Greg and her. Cass sighed and took a baked empanada onto a plate, cut it in half and topped one bite with one sauce, the other bite with a different one. "These are really good."

"So's this hamburger."

"Thanks. Our hamburgers are the best in Texas, second only to our chili."

"I love the chili here. I'll get that next time."

She tried a fried empanada and the other sauce, then left him to his meal. "See you in the morning about ten?"

He nodded.

Cass made a beeline for her mother and pulled her around a corner and out of sight. "What's the big idea?"

Gloria raised her eyebrows and feigned puzzlement. "I don't understand."

"Greg is my contractor. Nothing more."

"He's very handsome and seems quite nice."

"I prefer Griff."

Gloria heaved a theatrical sigh and walked away.

This wasn't good, Cass thought.

DURING THE AFTERNOON LULL, Cass retreated to her office to study the figures Greg had given her. She was impressed with his presentation and his estimate of the costs. Both were very complete and much more reasonable than the other contractor had offered for the same work. She compared the two carefully. Greg had also provided a list of stores and suppliers where he got builder discounts. Cass called him and told him the job was his.

Another call buzzed in as she was saying goodbye to Greg. It was Griff.

"Hi," she said. "How's Miami?"

"Nice, but I'd rather be in Austin."

"I'd rather you were here, too. I was just talking to my new contractor when you called. We're starting renovations on my houses on Monday."

"That was quick."

"Things happened to work out well. Are you coming back soon? You can help me move the POAC office. One of our members is donating office space in her building."

"When are you moving?"

"Either tomorrow or Sunday afternoon. I'll be working Saturday."

"Babe, I wish I could be there, but it looks like I'll be in Miami until Saturday, and I have some things to take care of in New York before I can leave. It will be at least Tuesday or Wednesday before I can wrap up my business and come home."

"Home? Are you thinking of Austin as home?"

"More and more," Griff said. "I told you I love the town. And Austin is where you are."

A big lump formed in her throat. "I miss you."

"I miss you more. Believe me, I'm doing everything I can to get there, sweetheart. You can't imagine. Cass, I love you so much."

She totally melted. There was no mistaking his words this time. She tried to say something, but her mouth wouldn't work.

"Cass?"

"Yes. I'm here. I—I…" The words just wouldn't come.

"Cass, I'm not rushing you, simply telling you how I feel."

"I understand," she said. And the tears came. She sniffed. Why was she crying? "I, uh, I can't talk right now."

"Sorry. I know you're working. I'll call you tomorrow night. Goodbye, sweetheart."

When the call ended, Cass put her head down and wept.

"Cass, honey, why are you upset?"

She looked up to see the Senator sitting across from her, looking concerned. Squeezing her eyes shut, she told herself she was hallucinating, but when she opened them again, he was still there.

"Griff told me he loves me."

"How wonderful! Don't you love him?"

"I—I'm not sure. We haven't known each other very long."

"Sometimes it doesn't take very long. The moment I saw your mother I fell head over heels for her. Now, *she* took a little longer to bring around."

Cass couldn't believe that she was sitting in the office calmly discussing her love life with a ghost. This was crazy.

As if he could read her mind, he smiled.

That made her more nervous. Still, she said, "Mom and Aunt Min don't like him."

"They didn't like me either, not at first. The important thing is not how they feel about him but how you feel. Listen to the quiet little voice deep inside you, and you won't go wrong."

"But—"

Just as quickly as he'd appeared, the Senator faded, and she was left talking to an empty chair.

Chapter Eighteen

Friday morning was a glorious day in Austin, with clear skies and with temperatures expected to be in the eighties. Dressed appropriately in shorts and sandals, Cass pulled to a stop in front of her house at exactly ten o'clock. Greg's big pickup was already there, and he was sitting on the front steps, waiting. Did his eyes linger a bit too long on her legs? If so, she didn't mind. In fact, she felt a little smug about still having good legs. She reminded herself it was past time to get back into her jogging routine. Monday for sure.

Hurrying up the broken concrete walk, she waved. "Am I late?"

"Nope. You're exactly on time." Clipboard in hand, he smiled and stood. "I'm a little early. Ready to measure?"

"I am." She held up her retractable tape. "Let me unlock the door. Karen isn't here today. We're hoping to find someone to move the office furniture today."

"I've been meaning to ask you about the office." He motioned toward the sign beside the front door. "Exactly what is POAC?"

"POAC stands for Preserve Old Austin's Charm. It's a non-profit organization that supports what its name implies. I'm the president." She told him a little bit about projects the group had been involved in.

"Cool," Greg said. "It breaks my heart when I see some of the landmarks torn down and paved over. I don't want Austin to become a city with a bunch of skyscrapers dominating the landscape."

Cass chuckled. "You sound like me. We'd love to have you as a member."

"Where do I sign up?"

She took a form from the filing cabinet. "Fill this out and send it in if you're truly interested."

"I am." He slipped the form into the papers on his clipboard. "Where is POAC moving?"

"To the building of one of our members, a couple of blocks over—if I can locate some muscle and a truck pretty soon."

"I've got some muscle and a truck. Is this all you have to move?" He motioned to the desk, folding chairs, a folding table and a file cabinet.

Cass looked around at the motley assortment of equipment and furniture and grinned. "This is it. Did I mention we keep the overhead low? Everything we have is either donated or bought from the Salvation Army store. We pay our secretary barely enough to keep her in gas money to work a few hours a week."

"I'll call two of my guys to come over, and by the time we're finished measuring, they'll have everything loaded up and ready to go."

"Oh, Greg, I hate for you to do that. I don't want to impose on your workers' time."

"Not a problem." Greg phone Chick, whoever he was, and told him to bring a couple of helpers to this address.

"That's very sweet of you, Greg."

He grinned. "I'm a sweet kind of guy. Let's use my tape." He unclipped an enormous tape measure from his belt and whipped it the length of the living room. "Sixteen." He moved and whipped it again. "Thirteen."

Cass hurriedly wrote down the numbers as he moved from room to room and called them out.

"Golly," she said when they were finished. "That took a whole five minutes. You're speedy."

He chuckled. "The other house had the exact same floor plan, so these same measurements should do for them. Let's talk about the fireplace. I assume you'd want it in the living room."

"Sure. I suppose another option would be between the living room and dining room." They walked back in that direction.

"It's a possibility, but it would cost considerably more. I recommend you put it right here between these two windows." He showed her several styles to choose from, then gave her a price for each.

"I love this one," Cass said, pointing out a contemporary one, faced with slate. "Let's do it."

"Good choice," he said. "A lot of people are putting their flat screen TVs over the fireplace. Want me to wire yours for a TV?"

"Great idea. How much will it cost?"

She was surprised at how little he quoted, and she scribbled the figure in her notebook a second before the helpers knocked on the front door. Greg instructed the two men on what to load in his truck, and while they were doing so, Cass called the owner of the new office space and told her they were on the way.

Greg drove the men and the furniture to the new site, and Cass followed behind. The furniture was moved and the office set up in less than an hour.

"I can't tell you how grateful I am for this, Greg," she told him warmly.

"Consider it my donation to POAC. Want to grab a bite of lunch at the place across the street?"

Cass hesitated. She rarely ate lunch so early.

"I wanted to go over some particulars about trim work and paint."

"Sure," she said. "I'm always up for Chinese. What about your men?"

"Chick will pick them up. He's on his way."

She and Greg walked across the street and went inside. It felt a little strange to be with another man and have him opening the door and touching her back to steer her to a table. Was she picking up some subtle signals or was he just another friendly guy?

After they ordered, he did indeed go over some ideas he had for the crown molding in both houses, as well as railings for the porches to make them look different from one another. He also suggested using reclaimed lumber. They decided on granite countertops for her house and concrete ones for the rental, and discussed interior molding colors.

When their food came, they put aside their respective notes and ate.

"Tell me," he said, "what have you been doing since high school?"

Cass briefly told him about college and law school and her stint as a lawyer in New York. "I stood it as long as I could, and then I headed back to Texas last year. I didn't like being a lawyer, and I missed home and my sister. What about you? As I recall, you had a football scholarship somewhere."

"I did. UCLA. I was studying architecture there, but I blew out my knee in my junior year. Surgery fixed me up to do everything except play football, and I dropped out of school. For a few years I knocked around California learning the building trades. Like you, I started missing Texas and my family, so I headed home a couple of years ago."

"Married? Children?"

He shook his head. "Nope. How about you?"

Cass had a feeling she needed to discourage any ideas of a personal relationship between them. "Nope. Me neither, but I've been seeing a very special guy. This may be the one."

"Then it wouldn't do me any good to ask you out on date?"

She smiled. "Sorry. I'm pretty sure my guy wouldn't approve."

"Well, damn. A day late and a dollar short. You know, I used to have a crush on you when you were a cute little sophomore cheerleader."

Cass laughed. "On Sunny or me?"

"Both of you, to tell the truth. I couldn't tell one from the other. But you seemed too young for me at the time."

"How funny. I figured you didn't know we were alive. So you never went back to get your architecture degree?"

He shook his head. "I kept putting it off for one reason or another, and now I'm too old."

"I don't think you're ever too old to go back to school."

"Maybe you're right, but I have people dependent on me now. My mom isn't in the best of health, and I support her and my special-needs sister."

While they finished lunch, Cass told him briefly about Sunny's life, as well. Greg was easy to talk to, and she really liked him, but the zing she felt with Griff simply wasn't there. She didn't have the slightest urge to jump across the table and nibble his ear or kiss him senseless.

Sorry, Mom.

SHE MISSED GRIFF dreadfully. Even though he called every day, it wasn't enough. Her days were busy and full, but still they seemed to drag by. When Sunny picked her up on Sunday morning to drive to Dripping Springs for their meeting with Carrie Outlaw, Cass welcomed the distraction of both having time alone with her sister and seeing Carrie.

Sunny drove like an old lady, but Cass didn't say a word about it as they tooled down the highway. This last time she'd come this way, Griff had been with her and nervous as a hooker in church about her heavy foot. She smiled, remembering.

"What?" Sunny said. "Why are you grinning like a possum in a persimmon tree?"

"I was thinking about something."

"Something or someone?" When she didn't answer, Sunny said, "Griff Mitchell, I'll bet. Are you getting serious about him, Cass?"

She sighed. "I think so, and it may be a problem. Mom and Aunt Min don't like him, and they can't explain why. How do you feel about him, sis?"

"He's good-looking for sure. And charming and thoughtful. But...I don't know, somehow I'm uneasy around him. Maybe it's the cop in me. Ben and Sam feel the same way. I'm not sure how Belle and her other brothers feel, but I know Sam ran a check on him."

Cass bolted straight up, and only her seat belt restrained her from shooting to her feet. Fury zipped through her like an express train. "Dammit! I can't believe he did that. Just because Griff doesn't have a Texas drawl doesn't mean he's a sleaze. Wait till I get my hands on Sam Bass Outlaw."

"Calm down, Cass. You're overreacting. Sam only did it

because he cares about you. Don't you want to know what he found out?"

She crossed her arms and stared straight ahead. "No! I wouldn't sink so low as to ask."

After a mile or two of silence, she relented. "Okay, what did Sam find out?"

"Griff was born on Long Island, went to Harvard, was the president of his class, also went to Harvard Law and graduated at the top of his class. He's licensed to practice law in New York, and his record is clean as a whistle except for a couple of speeding tickets and a disturbing the peace citation when he was in college."

"I could have told Sam all that and saved him a world of time and trouble. I can't believe he checked Griff out."

"Don't be angry, Cass. Maybe it's because none of us are used to being around rich folks from New Yawk, as you call it. You probably rubbed elbows with people like that when you lived there. We didn't. Sometimes you distrust what's not familiar. Maybe that's what we're feeling."

"Ben, too?"

Sunny nodded. "Sorry. And maybe J.J.," she added quietly.

"Has the *entire* family been discussing Griff and his 'slick' ways?"

"We aren't trying to be nosy. We care about you."

"Let's talk about something else," Cass said. "I saw the Senator again. Saw him, hell. We had a conversation."

Sunny glanced over at her with a surprised look. "You did?"

"I kid you not."

"What did you talk about?"

"He told me to listen to the quiet voice inside me and follow my heart."

"Then I'd pay attention to his advice if I were you," Sunny said. "He's never steered me wrong."

"Maybe so, but his flitting in and out like he does makes me nervous. And speaking of nervous," Cass said, thrumming her fingers against her thigh, "I'm itching to know what Carrie wants to talk with us about. Have you come up with any ideas?"

"Not a one. I suppose we're going to have to wait another few minutes to find out. Seems strange it's Carrie, of all people, who wants to talk with us. And privately."

"Well, she's a lawyer. But so's Frank. And Belle, too, for that matter."

"Here we are," Sunny said, turning in at their meeting place. "We'll soon find out."

Chapter Nineteen

Drops of rain began to pelt the windshield as they pulled into a parking space in front of the diner. Sunny grabbed a collapsible umbrella from the backseat, and they made a run for the door. No sooner were they inside with the bacon and coffee smells than thunder boomed and a torrent of rain washed from the sky, hammering the metal roof like pebbles.

Looking around, they spotted Carrie in a back booth. Smiling brightly, she rose and came to meet them. As always, Cass wondered at the amazing color of her eyes. They were a bright, stunning amethyst.

"Good to see you," Carrie said, hugging them in turn. "I was afraid you weren't going to make it before the rain. I swear the clouds chased me all the way from Wimberley."

"It was sunshiny and clear in Austin," Cass said.

"I hope it makes it up our way," Sunny added. "My flowers could use the rain."

Carrie led them back to the booth where she'd been sitting. "I'm having a cup of coffee already. Would you like some while we study the menu?"

"Absolutely," Cass said.

Carrie held up two fingers toward the waitress behind the

counter, and they soon had steaming cups in front of them.
"What's good here?" she asked as the waitress refilled her cup.

"Everything's good, but our migas are smokin'. Be right
back for your order."

"You know, as a Texan I hate to admit it, but I've never had
migas," Carrie said. "I often see them on menus. What are they?"

"Sort of Tex-Mex scrambled eggs, only better," Sunny told
her. "You start by sautéing small pieces of corn tortillas and
add onion and chilies and anything else you want, then
scramble all that with eggs beaten with a little cream or milk.
Melt cheese over that, and top it with salsa and cilantro."

"It's delish," Cass added. "And practically a staple in Austin."

"Sounds fattening," Carrie said. "I was going to have a
poached egg and fruit."

Cass grinned. "Come on, Carrie, live it up. You can have
it without chorizo or bacon to save calories."

Carrie agreed, and they all ordered the "smokin'" migas.

As soon as the waitress left, Cass said, "I know we should
ask about Frank and the kids and the rest of the family first,
but my curiosity is killing me. What in the world do you want
to talk to us about privately?"

"It's kind of heavy," Carrie said. "Maybe we'd better wait
until after the migas."

"Car-rie," Sunny said. "You can't leave us hanging like that."

"Sorry. You're right. Let me start at the beginning. You
know I used to be a landman for my uncle's oil company, and
I first went to Naconiche to lease property for drilling."

"Right," Cass said.

"Well, a lot of the property belonged to the Outlaw family.
It had come down from old Judge John Wesley Hardin Outlaw
to his two sons, Wes and Butch. Wes and his family were no
problem, but since Butch was dead, I located his recorded

will, and he'd left everything to his wife, Iris. I imagine the will was drawn up long before he met your mother."

Cass and Sunny looked at each other, and Cass wondered where this was going.

"Iris remarried and moved out of state. Nobody was quite sure where she relocated, but intrepid researcher that I am, I found her. She didn't want anybody in the family to know her whereabouts, so I agreed to keep all her information confidential."

"And she got the money?" Sunny said.

"Yes."

"So?"

The waitress returned with their order, and everybody dug into the tantalizing concoction, sensing perhaps that the migas might be less appetizing after Carrie's tale.

For a few moments, they ate without speaking. Finally Cass could stand it no longer and put down her fork. "Why are you telling us this?"

"Iris Outlaw Bradford, who had been widowed a second time, recently died. Her lawyer contacted me as per her instructions."

"And?"

"The bottom line is she left everything to the two of you."

"Good Lord!" Sunny's fork clattered to her plate. "Why?"

"I'm not quite sure," Carrie said. "From what I know about the situation, I would assume it was guilt for keeping your father from marrying your mother. I had a feeling that's why she left Naconiche."

"How much are we talking about here?" Cass said.

"A considerable amount. The will is being probated, but as far as I can tell, you own your father's part of the Outlaw land and the income from oil and gas production there. It's a rich site, and it will be producing for quite some time."

"Holy guacamole!" Cass said.

"I don't know any particulars about her personal estate yet, but her lawyer, who is her executor, indicated she was well-fixed."

"You mean we're rich?" Sunny said.

"At least quite comfortable. Or you will be as soon as the estate's settled. I was hoping it would be completed by this weekend so I could give you more particulars, but it will be another few days or perhaps weeks before everything can be turned over to you. Iris's attorney also sent me this letter to give to the two of you. Perhaps it will answer most of your questions." Carrie handed them the sealed envelope she'd taken from her bag.

The twin's names were typed across the front, along with "To be opened after my death."

Cass took it and used her knife as a letter opener. "Excuse us, Carrie. We can't wait any longer." She unfolded the pages and, holding them so Sunny could read, scanned the letter. Her mouth dropped open as she read. "Son of a bitch!" Anger boiled up hotter than molten lava.

"Wrong gender," Sunny said, "but I couldn't have said it better. I hope she rots in hell! I don't want her damned money!"

"She *murdered* our father!" Cass said to Carrie. "Shot him dead on the steps of the capitol building."

Sunny tapped the page with her finger. "She admits it right here. No wonder the bitch felt guilty!"

"Oh, dear God," Carrie said, covering her mouth. "I'm so sorry. I never imagined…"

Cass touched Carrie's arm. "No need to be sorry. We're not going to slay the messenger." She handed the pages to Carrie to read.

The migas lay congealing on their plates as they all three sat there, stunned by Iris's confession.

After a long silence, Sunny said, "Well, the case is finally closed. We'll have to tell Wes right away."

"Would you like me to tell him?" Carrie asked.

Sunny and Cass looked at each other, then nodded. "Please. I think we need some time to process this."

"I think you're right," Carrie said. "And don't be too hasty to refuse the money and land. After all, it was your father's birthright…and yours."

Cass nodded. "We need to wait until the estate is settled, and we have all the facts and some emotional distance from this." She fluttered the pages.

"You're right," Sunny said. "I feel like I ought to belly up to a bar and toss back a stiff one to settle my nerves, but I'd throw up. My stomach might never be the same again."

"I hear you," Cass said. "Carrie, I know you'll understand if we leave now. We have some concerns to discuss. We need some time to wrap our minds around this."

"I do understand. I wish I could do something to make the situation easier."

The waitress came over with the coffeepot and their check. "Something wrong with the migas?"

"The migas were superb," Cass said.

"I'll get the check," Carrie said. "Go ahead." She stood and hugged them both again.

THE RAIN SOON SLACKED off, and they ran out of it entirely as they drove back to Austin. Cass reread Iris's letter as they drove. Her initial anger had cooled a bit, and she struggled to study it with an objective mind. "'If you can't forgive me, at least I hope you'll pray for my tortured soul,'" she read aloud.

"You know, sis, I'm not nearly ready to forgive her, but I can sort of understand her. Our mother and father weren't exactly blameless in this situation. He was, after all, a married man."

"Cass, that doesn't excuse *murder.* And with his own damned gun! She deserved to be locked up in prison all these years."

"Spoken like a cop, but I agree."

"We have to report this, you know."

"To whom? And why? It's been over thirty years."

"I know," Sunny said, "but the authorities need to close the case."

"I suppose you're right, but I'm more concerned about telling Mom than about turning over Iris's confession to the police. Do you think we should tell her?"

"Eventually, but not now."

"I agree," Cass said. "Let's pick a better time. Do you wonder how Iris knew so much about us? I get the impression that she'd followed our lives to some extent."

"With the Internet, tracking down people is fairly easy."

"Now, sure, but widespread use of the Net is fairly recent."

"Who knows?" Sunny said. "Private detectives maybe. Or for all we know she may have dropped into Chili Witches now and then for a bowl of chili. Nobody would have recognized her. I don't think Mom or Aunt Min knew her from a hole in the wall."

Cass put the letter away and leaned her head against the seat rest. "I wonder if her second husband knew what she'd done. She was a tortured soul for sure."

"Cass, have you ever considered becoming a defense attorney? You're beginning to sound like one. I don't care if she was a tortured soul. She should have thought of the consequences before she pulled the trigger. I'm irritated because somebody from APD didn't haul her in and sweat a confession out of her. Every rookie knows to look at the spouse first."

"Tell the truth, Sunny. Did you ever think his wife did it?"

She sighed. "No. I always assumed it was politically moti-vated somehow. There were some hot issues at the time, and from what I've read, our dad made some enemies in the opposite camp."

When they arrived at Chili Witches, they decided to go into the office and make copies of Iris's letter, and that Sunny should keep the original in a lockbox at her house. Knowing the media would probably get hold of the story and splash it all over everywhere, they decided to hold off on turning the information over to the police. Maybe Sam could give them some ideas about how best to handle it. After all, Cass reminded her sister, they were under no legal obligation to report what they knew.

"Want to come upstairs?" Cass asked.

"No. I need to get home. Ben and Jay are dropping over later, and we're going to play miniature golf. Want to go?"

Cass rolled her eyes. "Surely you jest. No, I'm going upstairs to clean my closet and get my mind off this latest disaster. Or wax my legs. Or watch a sappy movie and cry a little bit." *And wish Griff was here.*

Sundays were very long when you didn't have someone to share them with.

HALFWAY THROUGH THE MOVIE, she ran out of tissues and had to resort to a roll of toilet paper tossed on the couch beside her. The movie, although it was a tearjerker, didn't account for all her weeping. Part of it was loneliness, part of it was sadness over the way her father had died. Part of it was general, wallowing misery over her current circumstances, a vague, amorphous blues. And part of it was probably feeling drained after the emotional day she'd had.

She turned off the television, hugged her knees to her chest and curled her bare toes over the edge of the couch cushion. Why couldn't life be simple?

Why didn't Griff call and lift her out of this mood?

Why was she waiting for him to call?

Picking up her cell, she punched in his number. It went directly to voice mail.

Damn. Where was he? Didn't he know she needed him? Tossing her phone aside, she rested her forehead on her knees and let the despair wash over her.

"Cass? All this will pass."

She glanced up to see her father sitting in a chair nearby. "Did you know that Iris shot you?"

"She was very hurt and angry. She felt embarrassed and betrayed. You mustn't resent her. Resentment becomes a festering sore inside you and poisons your whole being. In the end, your negative emotions accomplish nothing and hurt only yourself. Forgiveness is very healing."

"Did you know she died?"

"I did. She's very lost right now, but she'll get better. It would help if you and Sunny would accept her gift. It's part of her atonement, and I want you to have what's your birthright. We must all love one another, Cass."

"I know, but sometimes it's very difficult. I feel as if my life is in chaos lately."

"I understand." His voice was gentle, soothing.

"I love Griff."

The Senator smiled. "That's good."

"But Mom and Aunt Min don't like him at all, and I don't think Sunny or the rest of the family are too fond of him, either."

"Give them time. Everything is going to be all right."

"I wish I could believe that. I have this awful feeling of impending doom I can't seem to shake."

The Senator only smiled and began to fade, leaving behind a whispered, "Trust…"

Chapter Twenty

Tuesday night's business was brisk, and Cass was happy to see the last customer leave. The staff closed down Chili Witches, and as soon as the last employee was out the back door, Cass set the alarm and locked up. She wasn't looking forward to sleeping with her stuffed cat again, but hopefully Griff would be back tomorrow. Phone calls just weren't cutting it.

She started up the back stairs to her apartment, but saw a shadow at the top that didn't belong there. Her heart accelerated and her foot froze on the step. She didn't even have pepper spray. Beginning a slow retreat and keeping her eye on the shadow, she was preparing to scream bloody murder and run like hell.

"Cass, it's me."

"Griff?"

"Yep."

"Griff!" She ran up the stairs and threw herself into his arms. Their kiss nearly blistered her nail polish.

"Oh, babe." He held her face between his hands and kissed it all over. "I've missed you something crazy."

"When did you get back?"

"How long does it take to drive from the airport? Add five minutes to that."

"Why didn't you tell me you were coming home tonight?"

"I wanted to surprise you. Are you surprised? I finished up everything earlier today and took the first plane I could get out of New York." He kept kissing her face.

She began unbuttoning his shirt and pulling it from his pants.

"Let's go inside," he said, his voice hoarse.

Reluctantly, she stopped unbuttoning and fished her key from her jeans. She unlocked the door in record time and pulled him inside after her, barely pausing to shut the door.

He kissed her again, almost devouring her like a starving man. She went back to work on the buttons, equally as hungry for him.

He was shucking off her shirt when suddenly a blaring, raucous noise filled the room.

"Oh, my gosh! The alarm." Cass made a run for the control panel and turned it off just as her phone began to ring. As she grabbed the phone, someone started banging on the door and yelling her name.

"Sorry," she told the security company on the phone. "I forgot to turn off the alarm when I came in." She motioned for Griff to get the door as she gave the caller her code.

When Griff opened the door, Hank stood just outside, wearing nothing but shorts and pointing his service revolver.

"Don't shoot, Hank! Don't shoot," Cass shouted. "It's Griff and me. False alarm."

Hank lowered his gun. "Damn near gave me a heart attack. Hello, Griff. Cass." He grinned.

Cass, whose tee was up around her neck, stepped behind Griff, whose shirt was unbuttoned and half off. Thankfully, only a dim lamp illuminated her apartment.

Griff gave a curt nod, and, peeking around his shoulder, Cass said, "Hello, Hank. Sorry to disturb you."

Still grinning, he said, "Aren't you going to invite me in for coffee?"

"You're not dressed," Griff mumbled.

Cass snorted and giggled, burying her face against Griff's back.

"Right," Hank said. His grin didn't falter. "Another time."

Griff closed the door in his face and turned back to Cass. "Now where were we?"

She stripped off her tee and threw her arms around his neck. "About here, I think."

His lips met hers, his tongue plunged into her mouth, and she went went wild in his arms.

"Oh, how I've ached for you," he whispered as he walked her backward to the couch.

"My bed is much more comfortable," she said, taking him by the hand and heading that way.

She nearly fell, hopping and pulling and trying to get her jeans off.

He steadied her, and they laughed.

"We have all night," Griff said. "No need to hurry."

"Maybe you don't need to, but I do. I'm dying here." Hopping again, she yanked off one shoe, then the other.

"We can't have that." He unhooked her bra, tossed it aside and toed off his own shoes. He bent and took a nipple into his mouth.

She moaned at the sensation. "Oh, Griff."

"Yes, love?"

"Do that again."

He went to the other breast, nipping and tasting as he hooked his thumbs in her panties and lowered them for her to step out of. His hands stroked up her legs, and one eased into the juncture.

She almost went through the ceiling with his intimate probing. "Don't!" she cried. "Stop." But he continued.

She went through the ceiling and shot to the stars as she throbbed around his fingers with spasm after spasm.

Gasping for breath, she laid her head against his shoulder. "I'm sorry. I told you to stop."

"I thought you said 'don't stop.' And anyhow, there's nothing to be sorry about, Cass. Not with me. Ever." He kissed her gently.

Her desire still wasn't sated. She longed for him as strongly as ever. Writhing and rubbing her breasts against his chest, she unhooked and unzipped his pants, feeling his hardness.

With swift motions, he stripped off his pants and backed her to the bed. They fell onto the mattress, and she clamped her legs around his waist.

"Oh, babe," he groaned. "You set me on fire."

He plunged deeply into her, and she cried out with pleasure. "I love you so much," she murmured into his ear.

Griff went even wilder. Like a force of nature, he plunged deeper, harder, and she clung to him as he took her to the top again. Her breasts swelled and her womb ached. She could feel him throb and begin to pump into her, and she came again. It was glorious. Beyond glorious. Beyond anything she'd ever felt. It went on and on and on.

"Holy guacamole," she gasped.

He was still a moment, then he began to laugh.

"Ooooh."

"Exactly."

SOMETIME IN THE MIDDLE of the night, Cass jerked upright in bed. "Ohmygod!"

"'S matter, honey?" Griff mumbled.

"We didn't use any protection."

He rolled over. "Would it be so bad if you got pregnant?"

"You're asking someone who was ridiculed for being a bastard? Of course it would be bad. I wouldn't do that to a child."

"If we got married, it wouldn't be a problem."

"Married?" she squeaked. "Are you out of your ever lovin' mind? We just met. I don't know you well enough to even discuss marriage. We're only up to the *L* word, and that seemed rushed. Forget the *M* word."

"Oh, I don't know," he said, stroking her tummy. "I think we know each other pretty well." He sounded amused.

"I'm not speaking of knowing in the biblical sense. I'm talking about the deeper sense, the psychological and spiritual sense. Why, I don't even know your favorite color."

"Blue. Yours?"

"Red and blue and yellow. And some greens. And I love teal."

"Doesn't that cover everything?" he asked.

"Oh, no. I'm not wild about most browns, mustard and magenta. And I don't much care for lime-green or dark olive."

"What's magenta?"

"It's kind of like fuchsia, only darker and less vivid."

He chuckled. "Of course. How could I not have known?" He kissed her nose. "Cass, I don't need a long time to know I'm wild, crazy in love with you. I've known a fair number of women in my life, and none of them came close to affecting me the way you do. Your smile lights me inside, and the sound of your voice sets my heart racing. Just being around you makes me feel as if I could fly."

She touched his cheek. "That's the sweetest thing anyone has ever said to me. But I want to make sure the feelings last. To me, marriage isn't on a trial basis. It's a lasting commitment."

"All I can say is every day I've known you, my feelings for you have grown. There's nothing I wouldn't do to make you happy. Nothing." He took her hand and kissed her fingers. "Nothing." He tucked her head against his shoulder. "Now go back to sleep and don't worry. You need your rest."

"Okay, but tomorrow I'm going to get a prescription for the pill. And let's not forget protection again. All right?"

"I promise."

Cass slept better than she had in days.

When she opened her eyes, Griff was on his side, head propped in his hand, watching her. She stretched and smiled.

He leaned over and circled her nipple with his tongue, then sucked gently. "I've been wanting to do that for the last twenty minutes."

"How long have you been awake?"

"Twenty minutes." He moved to the other breast, blowing gently, then taking the hardened tip into his mouth. "Mmm."

"Mmm, yourself. I have to brush my teeth and take a shower."

"Sometimes hygiene is highly overrated." His attention went back to her breast.

"Not in my book."

"Do you have an extra toothbrush?"

"Where's yours?"

"In my luggage. In my car. Out front. Be still."

"Griff, I'm getting up. Let go. Ouch!"

"Sorry. Let me kiss it and make it well."

She laughed and twisted away, batting him with her pillow. "I've got first dibs on the bathroom. Why don't you make coffee?"

Considerably refreshed, she came out of the bathroom a few minutes later, to smell coffee brewing and see Griff headed toward her, naked as a jaybird.

"Where are your clothes?" she asked, trying not to stare at some of his more magnificent parts.

"In a wrinkled mess on the floor. Be right back." He kissed her on the way to the bathroom.

"I left a new toothbrush out on the counter," she called after him.

His clothes were indeed a wrinkled mess. She tossed them on the bed, then got out her ironing board and set the iron to heating while she dressed in capris and a cool, sleeveless top. By the time Griff exited the bathroom with a towel draped around his hips, his pants were pressed and she was steaming the last sleeve of his shirt.

"What are you doing?" he asked.

"Haven't you ever seen anybody iron?" she countered.

"You're ironing my clothes?"

"Why is that such a surprise?" She held up his shirt. "It's no big deal. I've been doing it most of my life."

His brows went up. "Ironing men's clothes?"

"No. Ironing *my* clothes." She smiled and held the shirt for him to slip his arms into. "I suppose the concept might be difficult to understand for a man who sends bathing suits to the laundry." She nipped his shoulder, then slid his shirt into place. "I'll go check on the coffee. I'm craving caffeine."

While Griff finished dressing, she went into the kitchen and poured two cups. She emptied a packet of sweetener in hers and took a sip. Not bad.

Joining her at the counter, Griff asked, "How's the coffee?"

"Quite good."

"Don't seem so surprised. I do have a few bachelor survival skills. It helps that we have the same brand of coffeemaker."

"Small world."

He wrapped his arms around her and grinned. "No, babe. It's kismet."

She snorted. "It's coincidence. Kismet is concerned with

weightier things. And don't expect me to make meaningful conversation until I've had my second cup of coffee."

"Got it." He opened the fridge. "What's for breakfast? Got any eggs?"

"Nope. Today is grocery day. You can have cereal or yogurt."

"Where's the milk?"

"Oops. You can have yogurt." She looked in the bread box. "And cinnamon raisin toast."

"I'll make the yogurt," he said, "and you make the toast. Orange or peach?" He held up two containers.

"Since you're the guest, you pick." She stuck two slices of slightly hard bread into the toaster. "Grab the butter while you're there."

He put the tub on the table and ripped off the yogurt tops while she set out plates, napkins and tableware. When the toast popped up, she put a slice on his plate and hers, and stuck two more pieces in the toaster.

Holding her chair while she seated herself, he nuzzled her neck. "See how well we work together? A perfectly coordinated meal with all the food groups."

Cass chuckled. "This probably isn't an adequate test. How are you on pot roast or fried chicken?"

"We can order in." He sat down, smeared butter on his toast and took a big bite. "Excellent, my dear. Excellent."

She laughed. "You're crazy."

"What are your plans for the day—besides grocery shopping?"

"I'd planned to go for a run this morning, but I think I'll skip it today."

"*Au contraire,* my dear. I think a jog along the lake would be a splendid idea. As soon as we've eaten, I'll go get my gear and join you."

"Au contraire?" She smirked at him.

"I had two years of French."

"So did I, but I rarely say *au contraire.*"

"Me either. In fact, I don't recall ever having the occasion to say it. What shall we do after we jog and buy groceries?"

"I want to go by and see what progress Greg has made."

"Greg?" His left eyebrow went up. "Who's Greg?"

"The contractor who's renovating my houses."

"Oh, okay. I'd like to go with you." Griff scraped the last bite of yogurt from his carton. "And sometime today I need to find a place to live. Any chance I can move in with you?"

Stunned, she stared at him as if he'd lost his cotton-pickin' mind.

Chapter Twenty-One

"Not a snowball's chance in hell," Cass said. "You are *not* moving in with me. As a matter of fact, I need to get you out of here before my mom and aunt show up and start asking questions."

"They're coming here?" Griff said.

"Not to my apartment, but they'll be in to help with the rush hour at Chili Witches. It makes them feel useful."

Griff looked as if he wanted to say more, but, bless him, he didn't argue. He merely shrugged. "It was worth a shot. You going to eat the rest of your toast?"

"Help yourself. Aren't you going back to the hotel?"

"No. Since I'm going to be here so much, I want to look at some longer term options."

She hesitated. "Longer term as in how long?"

"That depends on you."

"No, don't base your decisions on me. Do what you want to do."

"Okay. I need someplace in Austin to live for a while. Any ideas?"

"I know a couple of real estate agents who may handle some rentals. Anita is on the board at POAC, and Diane is Hank Wisda's sister."

"Hank? The cop next door with the gun?"

"Yes, she's less threatening than Hank."

"Let's call both and see what furnished places they might have available."

Cass made the calls. Anita didn't have anything suitable, but Diane had two or three condos she thought might do, and she could show them right away. "Want to skip the jog?"

"Yes. If I can't stay here, I'd like to have a closet to hang my clothes."

"Don't pull Mr. Pitiful on me, buster," she said, laughing. "Your car or mine?"

"Let's take mine. I'm parked at a meter outside, and I don't want to get a ticket."

"Let's boogie." Cass grabbed her purse and they went downstairs. When they reached Griff's rental car, she laughed and pointed to the windshield. "Too late."

Looking disgusted, Griff pulled the ticket from his car. "And here I thought I was getting into the Austin spirit by renting a hybrid. Think Hank can get it fixed for me?"

"I wouldn't count on it. Pay the fine. It's probably only fifteen bucks, and you can pay online or by phone. What's all that?" she asked, peering into the backseat at two large boxes.

"Some things that wouldn't fit in the trunk."

"Where's your luggage?"

"In the trunk."

Puzzled, she shrugged. "Whatever floats your boat." Those suckers must have cost a fortune to bring on the plane. She gave him directions to Diane's office.

Diane, a little red-haired dynamo with a big smile, arranged for them to see three places, starting with the most distant. The first, a two-bedroom condo on the west side, with a lake view and nice furnishings, Griff said was too far out of town.

The next was in the Hyde Park area, and the furniture was Victorian with crocheted antimacassars. Cass bit back a laugh when Griff looked horrified and said, "Not exactly my style."

The last one was a two-bedroom corner unit in a downtown high-rise, with a spectacular view of both the capitol and the lake. Its contemporary furnishings were something out of *Architectural Digest*.

"The owners of this unit," Diane said, sweeping her hand toward the open living area, "spend several months a year in Canada to be near their grandchildren. They left just three days ago, so the place is available for up to four months. It's actually a three-bedroom unit, but the smallest bedroom is used to store their personal items. Covered parking downstairs and valet service is included, as is weekly maid service."

"I'll take it," Griff said.

"Don't you want to see the rest of the condo?"

"Sure, but I'll take it. When can I move in?"

"Wouldn't you like to know the price?" Diane asked.

She named a price and Cass flinched. Griff said, "I'll take it."

"Fantastic," Diane said. "Let's go back to my office and do the paperwork, and I'll give you the key."

As they were walking out, Griff put his arm around Cass's waist. "Don't you like this place?"

"It's beautiful. But there used to be a stable and a blacksmith shop on this site. A shame."

"Cass," he said gently, "nowadays I don't think there's much call for a stable or a blacksmith in downtown Austin."

She smiled. "You're right, of course. So I'll excuse you for living here."

"Good. I don't think I could take all those little lace doilies."

AFTER THE PAPERS WERE signed and the money was paid, they stopped for lunch, then headed to Griff's new home to drop off his belongings.

"We'll need the trunk space for groceries later. Not only yours, but mine. I'll need everything. Did you notice if there was a coffeemaker there?"

"I think so, but we can check when we go by. Griff, you haven't stopped smiling. What's up?"

"I'm happy." He reached for her hand and squeezed it. "Happy to be here, happy to be with you. Happy."

She smiled. His words were like a soft, cuddly hug, and she reveled in the feeling. She was happy, too.

"Have you heard any more about your inheritance?"

"Nothing yet. Carrie said it might be a while yet." She'd discussed the entire situation with Griff on the phone, so he was aware of Iris's letter and her will. "Carrie called Sunny yesterday, and told her she'd spoken to Wes and Nonie about the murder. Frank knows as well, but they all decided to wait and let us tell the others in our own time."

"Good idea. How did Wes take it?"

"In stride, the way he takes everything. Said after all the years he spent as sheriff, nothing much surprises him. He was pleased about Sunny and me getting Iris's estate. I believe his exact words were 'Fair enough.'"

They pulled into the underground parking garage, and Griff spoke to someone at the valet stand for a few minutes. A man soon came out with a dolly and loaded on boxes and some of the luggage. Griff took two large rolling bags and Cass took a smaller one and his laptop case.

"Did you bring everything you own?" she asked.

"Yep, almost. A few things are being shipped later. Most I sold."

Though blown out of the water by what Griff said, she held her questions until they were upstairs and the helper had been tipped and left.

"I don't understand," Cass said. "What did you sell?"

"Just stuff I don't need anymore. Things which were more trouble and expense to move than they're worth. My apartment. The furniture. My car."

"But why?"

His dimples flashed as he put both arms around her waist. "I told you I was considering a move to Austin. Well, now I've moved. Want to go check out the king-size bed in the master?"

"No, I have questions. First I want to know—"

He kissed her, and the questions burning inside her went down in flames. All she could say was, "Mmm."

LATER, MUCH LATER, THEY showered and dressed, having left the bed thoroughly initiated. Griff wore shorts, a T-shirt and flip-flops.

Cass looked him up and down as they waited for the elevator. "Way to go."

"I feel a little underdressed."

"Naw. You'll get used to it."

"Will my toes get used to these thongs?"

"Sure, they'll toughen up. What's in the bag?" She pointed to the small duffel he carried.

"Running shorts and shoes."

"For running or to wear if your toes give you grief?"

He grinned. "Got me."

They drove to her houses to check out the renovations. Cass noticed Greg's truck there, and Griff pulled in and parked behind it.

When they got out, she shaded her eyes and looked up. "Wow, the new roof is almost finished."

Greg came down the steps. "The roofers will finish it up tomorrow and may get the one next door done as well." He held out his hand to Griff. "Greg Gonzales."

"Griff Mitchell."

"We're hoping to get a new roof on mine before we have rain."

"Yours?" Griff asked. "You buy one of these houses?"

"Buying. Good investment I lucked into. Mine is that one down on the corner. I'll either rent it out or resell it." To Cass he said, "There's not much to see inside. We're demolishing the kitchen and baths. Did you get the tile picked out?"

"I did. I left all the information with Reuben at the tile store. And on Friday I'll make my final decision about cabinets and fixtures, and let you know."

"Good."

Two men came out of the house carrying an old sink and countertop, and tossed them into a big Dumpster between the two houses.

"We're about to knock off," Greg told them. "If you go inside, be careful where you step. Things are a mess."

"We'll wait for another time," she said. "I just love to watch the progress."

Greg gave a two-finger salute and walked back in the house.

"Seems like a nice guy," Griff said.

"He is. We went to school together. He played football at UCLA for a while. I hadn't seen him for years until people recommended him for his job, and I contacted him. He's even joined POAC."

"You don't say. Guess I'll have to sign up, too."

"Only if you want to. Ready to go grocery shopping? You need to stock up."

"I don't need much," he said.

Famous last words.

They laughed their way through the produce section as Griff piled some of every fruit in the store his cart, along with salads and potatoes. He was in heaven when the found they gourmet soup section. At the meat counter, he selected four giant rib eye steaks.

"Four?" Cass asked.

"I like steak. You think I can't cook? I'll cook you a steak tonight."

"Deal."

He went up and down the aisles, tossing stuff in his basket like a contestant on *Supermarket Sweep*. By the time he was finished, his cart was piled high, while Cass had only eggs, bread, peanut butter, coffee and milk in hers. And two oranges.

"We'd better go by your place and stow your things first," Cass said when they were loading his car. "All that ice cream is going to melt. I don't understand why you got so much."

"I like ice cream."

"But *four gallons?*"

"Ah, sweetie, don't sweat it." He gave her a peck as he heaved another sack into the trunk.

Back at his condo, the valet helped tote the groceries upstairs, and soon everything was put away. Cass reminded Griff that her eggs and milk were still in the car and needed to get into her fridge right away.

"You can bring your things up here," he said. "Remember, I'm going to cook steaks for you."

"How about we do the steaks another night? Let's drop my stuff off, and I'll buy you a bowl of chili. I need to make an early night of it. I have paperwork to do. We've decided to move forward with the frozen chili deal."

"Great. Does this mean you can retire from the café?"

"Why would I want to retire?" She drilled his belly with her finger. "Come on, cowboy, move it. My eggs are going to hatch."

"Let me change my shoes first. These flip-flops are a bitch."

WHEN THEY WALKED INTO Chili Witches, the first person Cass saw was her mother. *Oh, crap.* Seemed that Gloria and Min had insisted Sunny take the night off to go to Jay's school pageant.

Gloria turned to Griff and gave him an anemic smile. "How are you this evening, Mr. Griffith?"

"Fine, thank you."

"His last name is Mitchell, Mom. *Griffin* is his first name."

"Oh, I'm so sorry, Mr. Mitchell. How very silly of me. I don't know where my mind is sometimes."

Cass rolled her eyes. Her mother was acting like that crazy Blanche in *A Streetcar Named Desire.* Which was not her style. At all. She was playing the passive-aggressive card, and Cass wanted to strangle her big time.

"I understand," he said. "Just call me Griff."

"We dropped off my groceries and decided to stop by and eat," Cass said.

"How wonderful. Would that table do?" Gloria pointed to one in the corner, as if Cass didn't know the layout of the place down to the last saltshaker.

"That table is perfect," Griff said to Gloria. "Could you join us?"

Cass kicked him in the ankle.

"Oh, how very sweet of you to ask, Mr. Griffith, but I'm much too busy working. And I wouldn't want to intrude."

Griff opened his mouth, and Cass kicked him again. Harder. "Another time, Mom. Would you send someone over with a couple of beers?"

When they were seated, Griff leaned over and asked quietly, "Does your mother have memory problems?"

"Nope. She's sharp as a tack. Sharper."

"I was afraid of that. I don't think she likes me."

Cass was trying to think of an appropriate response without flat out lying when Gloria came sashaying over with two draft beers on a tray. She tripped—quite theatrically, Cass thought—and dumped both foaming mugs smack in Griff's lap.

Chapter Twenty-Two

Horrified, Cass watched Griff's eyes widen, but he didn't say a word.

"Mother!" Cass grabbed a handful of napkins.

"Oh, dear merciful heavens, Mr. Griffith, I'm so sorry. Don't move. I'll get some towels. Jeff! Bring towels!" she shouted over her shoulder.

With the yelling, customers who'd missed the original catastrophe added their stares to the others who were gawking at the beer dripping from Griff's lap onto the floor.

"Oh, Mr. Griffith, can you ever forgive me? Sometimes my arthritis acts up, and I get so clumsy."

"What arthritis?" Cass said. "You don't have arthritis."

"Don't worry about it, Ms. O'Connor," Griff said. "Accidents happen. My mom has arthritis, and sometimes her hands bother her, as well."

"Well, bless your heart, Mr. Griffith. Aren't you the sweetest thing. Here, Jeff's brought some towels. Let me help you clean up." She began dabbing at his lap.

"I think I can handle it," he said, looking pained as he grabbed the towels from Gloria.

If Cass hadn't been so ticked off at her mother, she would

have laughed. "Let's go upstairs to my apartment, Griff, and you can shower. I'll wash your clothes and put them in the drier."

It was her mother's turn to look horrified. Good enough for her.

Griff nodded and tried to dry off as best he could. When he rose, he laughed and said loudly enough for all the gawkers to hear, "Sorry about the interruption, everybody. Dessert is on me." He glanced down at his lap. "As is my beer."

Everybody laughed along with him.

"Mother," Cass muttered between clenched teeth. "We'll talk later."

She and Griff hurried out the back way and up to her apartment.

"Griff, I'm so sorry. I don't know what got into my mom. This isn't like her."

"Don't worry, honey. Accidents happen." He stripped off his clothes and handed them to her.

"You know and I know that what happened was no accident. Why would Mom do such a thing? I'm so embarrassed."

"Don't be. For some reason she doesn't like me, and she's a lioness protecting her cub. Give me some time. I'll bring her around." He gave Cass a peck on the nose. "Would you get my gym bag from the car?"

"Sure. And I'll call downstairs and have our food delivered up here."

"Mind if we skip the chili tonight? I've lost my taste for chili and beer."

GRIFF DECIDED TO GO back to his condo and leave Cass to her work. She wondered if it wasn't merely a polite kiss-off. No, he was sincere, she told herself, when he'd said it would take more than a little beer to get rid of him for good.

He might be polite and forgiving, but Cass was royally pissed at her mother, and she stomped downstairs to confront her. Aunt Min saw her come in, and hurried to meet her.

"Oh, Cass, I'm so sorry about what happened. Did Griff leave?"

"Naturally. Were you a part of the floor show?"

"Absolutely not! I was in the kitchen."

"Where's Mom?"

"Hiding in the office. Are you angry?"

"Of course I'm angry." Cass wheeled and strode to the office.

Her mother was sitting behind the desk, her head in her hands. She didn't look up when Cass slammed the door. "Why, Mom? *Why?* And don't feed me any bull about accidents or arthritis or poor memory."

When Gloria looked up, her eyes were red-rimmed and teary. "I—I don't want you to get hurt, Cass. I'll do whatever it takes to keep that from happening. I don't trust him. I never have. From the first moment I met him, I knew he was up to something. Something deceptive. He's using you for his own purposes. Mark my words, the man's a charlatan."

Cass rolled her eyes. "And what are you? Psychic?"

Her mother took a deep breath and stared directly into Cass's eyes.

"Yes. As a matter of fact, yes, I am."

Cass knees gave way and she plopped down in a chair. "Since when?"

"Since as long as I can remember. I screamed and fainted the moment your father was shot. Ask Min. I'd been uneasy for several days before it happened. I get feelings."

"And you're *never* wrong?"

"Rarely. I'm not wrong about this."

"But, Mom, Sam Outlaw checked him out. He's clean."

"And exactly why did Sam, a *Texas Ranger,* check him out?"

Cass squirmed. "Bad vibes? I don't know."

"I'll bet Sam didn't trust him, either."

"Perhaps not, but I trust him, Mom. I love Griff."

"Oh, dear God!"

"Mom, cut the dramatics."

"Will you promise me, promise me sincerely that you'll find out more about him before you do something foolish?"

Cass wondered what her mother considered foolish. She'd already done everything except elope with him. "If it will ease you mind, Mom, I promise."

"Oh, thank you, dear. Thank you." She hurried from behind the desk and bent over to hug Cass. "Do it right away. I've been having such bad feelings." She kissed Cass's forehead and held her close in the comforting and protective way she'd always done.

"I will, Mom."

CASS SAT IN FRONT OF her computer for the longest time, indecision eating her from the inside out. Did she trust Griff or not? She'd trusted Daniel, and look where it got her. Her father had told her to follow her heart, but then he was a ghost, and she'd promised her mother, who was flesh and blood.

Oh, hell and damnation! It was a simple matter to type his name into the search engine. Checking the Internet was no big deal. It was a wonder she hadn't done it sooner.

G-r-i-f-f-i-n M-i-t-c-h-e-l-l

She punched "Search," closed her eyes and waited.

All kinds of Griffin Mitchells popped up, including a sixteen-year-old in Anaheim who was on Facebook, and one who had died recently in Alabama. The only ones she found for *her* Griffin Mitchell were innocuous mentions of information she already knew about.

Her shoulders slumped in relief. Should she take it further?

In for a penny, in for a pound.

Cass picked up her cell and punched in Maddie Evert's number.

When her friend and former colleague answered, she said, "Hey, Maddie, this is Cass. How are things in the Big Apple?" They yakked for a few minutes before Cass jumped in. "I have a big favor to ask. I know you went to Harvard. Did you happen to know a Griffin Mitchell? I'm not sure of the year he was there, but I'd guess he was ahead of you."

Maddie didn't know him, but suggested her older brother or cousin might. Both were Harvard educated lawyers in New York.

"Would you check around for me and find out anything you can about him? Confidentially, please. It's, uh, business, and I want to know who I'm up against."

Maddie agreed to ask around and call back when she heard something.

When Cass hung up, she felt slightly dirty.

More than slightly.

She took a deep breath and tried to let it go.

Looking through the stack of business mail she needed to answer, she couldn't believe they'd received another letter from Walter Zeagler, the guy in New York who was so hot to buy the Chili Witches tract. Slicing it open, she was a bit surprised that not only had her last response not discouraged him, but he was requesting a meeting with them the following week. Why was ZASM Consulting so interested in their property?

Although she was certain what they would say, Cass set the letter aside to discuss with the family, and turned to other correspondence. She stopped only to have a peanut butter sandwich and a glass of milk, and by eleven she was finished and fell into bed.

But she couldn't sleep. Her sheets smelled of Griff.

She ran her fingers over the spot where he had slept, and hugged his pillow close, breathing in the tantalizing scent of him. She loved him so. Her mother couldn't be right about him. She just couldn't.

A small voice inside her seemed to whisper, "He loves you, truly loves you."

She had to believe that.

TOWARD THE TAIL END of rush hour, Cass looked up from the register to see Griff by the front door talking to Aunt Min. He held three smallish boxes tied with red ribbons, and she watched him present one to Min with a big smile. Cass looked around for her mother, but she must have been in the kitchen or office.

"Hi there," Cass said, walking toward him.

"Hello yourself. I got a yen for some chili." He handed her a box.

"He gave me one, too," Aunt Min said, holding open a box of chocolate-covered strawberries and smiling brightly. "Aren't they scrumptious looking?"

"Where's your mom?" Griff asked. "I have one for her as well."

"I'll go see if I can locate her," Min said. "You can seat Griff."

When her aunt left, he said, "At least she got my name right."

"Aunt Min is a dear." Cass motioned to a small table by the window. "Want a beer?"

"After last night, I'm not sure I'll ever want another beer. Do you have time to join me?"

"I'll take a few minutes. We're not too busy."

They had a quiet lunch, but Gloria never showed her face. After Griff left, Cass took the other box and tracked her mother down in the office. "Griff brought this for you."

"Oh, thank you, dear." She set the box on the desk without even peeking inside.

Later, after Min and Gloria had left for the day, the box still sat on the desk.

Cass sighed. What a mess. She was too old to play Juliet.

AFTER SHE CLOSED, Cass again found Griff waiting for her on the steps to her apartment. "What are you doing here?" she asked.

"I was lonely. Pack a bag and come with me. I've bought bubble bath and more massage oil. I'll rub your feet. And we'll spend all day tomorrow feeding each other bananas and grapes."

"Bananas and grapes?"

"Somebody has to eat all the fruit I bought. And I'll cook you the steak I promised."

Cass had to consider for only half a second. She tossed some things in an overnighter and they were off.

"Do you like Marcia Ball?" he asked.

"I adore Marcia Ball. She's won blues awards out the kazoo."

"Good. I heard phenomenal things about her and got tickets to her show at someplace called Antone's tomorrow night."

"Great. Antone's is a nightclub on Fifth Street."

When they arrived at his building, Griff carried her bag upstairs. "Want a glass of wine while I fix your bath?"

"I'd love a glass of wine, but you don't have to fix my bath."

"Don't be so independent. Let me do this for you. Red or white?"

"White."

He filled two glasses and handed one to her. "I'll be right

back." He flipped something and soft sax music drifted through the apartment. "Great sound system here."

In a few minutes he returned, picked up her wine and pulled her to her feet. "Your bath is drawn." He led her into his big spa-like bathroom, where a dozen candles perfumed the air and bubbles almost spilled out of the tub. "I overestimated the bubble bath a little, but I think this will do. Hop in. I'll be right back."

Cass didn't have to be asked twice. She quickly shed her clothes and stepped in.

And quickly stepped out. The water was scalding hot, and her toes were boiled. She began to add some cold, but the bubbles rose higher and higher like a giant soufflé over the rim of the tub. She scooped a huge armload of foam and looked around for a place to put it.

The only logical place was the shower.

She was on her third armload when the door opened.

"What are you doing?" Griff asked.

"Moving bubbles. Help me. They're alive and multiplying." She handed him her load and reached for another.

"Honey, turn off the faucet."

"I can't find it!"

Mounds of bubbles were spilling onto the floor when Griff waded through the mess and managed to turn off the water. Hands on his hips and a disgusted expression on his face, he surveyed the foam covering the bathroom and spat out a very succinct expletive.

Cass picked up a big bunch of foam, shaped it into a huge ball and began singing "A Pretty Girl Is Like a Melody" as she danced around the room.

Griff grinned, then began to laugh until they were both roaring. He hugged her to him, squashing her ball. "Cass, you're one of a kind. And how I love you!"

Chapter Twenty-Three

Griff had to chuckle. Cass had insisted on taking the bath he'd prepared for her, and they'd finally herded enough of the foam into the shower stall for her to do so. Towels lined the floor, capturing the rest of the mess, and Cass lay, her head on a plastic pillow, surrounded by slowly diminishing bubbles, sound asleep. He knew she must be exhausted.

He knelt by the tub and kissed her. "Babe?"

"Hmm?"

"You have to wake up. You're getting wrinkly."

She opened her eyes. "Was I asleep?"

"You were. Come on. I'll help you dry off."

Between the two of them, they managed to get her dry, and he wrapped his robe around her and carried her to bed. Before he could undress and join her, she'd curled up and was sound asleep again.

He eased in under the sheets, feelings of protective tenderness filling his heart to near bursting.

He'd heard sappy love songs forever, but for the first time in his life he understood the meaning behind all of them. Heart and soul, she was the one. Whatever it cost him, Cass was worth it. He wanted to slay dragons and lay the world at her feet, and God help anyone who ever hurt her. Moreover, he wanted to rip out his tongue and stomp on it for ever agreeing to romance her out of Chili Witches. Griff had gotten caught in his own trap, and ZASM had been the biggest dragon of all.

CASS PURRED AND STRETCHED in bed like a satisfied cat. Nothing was quite as nice as making love in the morning. She rolled over onto her side and glanced at the clock. It was after nine, and she didn't care. She and Griff had all day to do nothing but eat, sleep and make love. How glorious. She stretched again, wondering if she should go join him in the shower.

On the nightstand a cell phone rang, and she automatically leaned over to look at the caller ID. *ZASM.* Walter Zeagler again. How did that jerk get her phone number?

Then it dawned on her. The phone wasn't hers. It was Griff's. What the—

Cass yanked up the phone. "Hello."

"Honey, let me talk to Griff."

A rock landed in her stomach, and horror spread over her like an alien blob. Bile rose up in her throat as things began to click into place. *Oh, no. Please, God, no.* She closed her eyes, hoping against hope…

"And who may I say is calling?" she asked as sweetly as she could manage.

"Tell him it's Walt, Walt Zeagler."

"And what is this in reference to, Mr. Zeagler?"

"Look, I'm his partner. He'll know what it's about. Now shake your tail, sweet-cheeks."

Click. The guillotine dropped. Fury rolled over her in tsunami waves. "Kiss my ass!" She hung up and turned off his phone. Not again! Dammit, not again!

She strode to the kitchen, poured three bottles of beer into the ice bucket and stomped back to the bathroom. Griff was just turning off the shower when she got there.

She jerked open the door. As he turned to her and smiled, she screamed, "You son of a bitch! You egg-sucking, lily-livered, low-down, slithering son of a bitch!" and heaved the beer and ice in his face. "If I had a knife, I'd gut you like a fish!"

Dropping the bucket, she ran from the room and slammed the door behind her. If she hadn't been naked as a jaybird, she'd have kept going, but she stopped to grab a pair of shorts and a T-shirt.

"Cass! Wait!" Griff charged from the bathroom, dripping water and swiping a towel over his face. "What's wrong?" He grabbed her arm.

She snatched it away. "Don't you touch me, you conniving scumbag." Not bothering with underwear, she yanked on the shorts and tee. "Don't you ever touch me again. Not ever!"

"Honey, whatever's wrong, I'll fix it. Just tell me why you're so upset."

"Walt Zeagler called while you were in the shower. We chatted."

Griff paled.

"Uh-huh." She snatched up her shoes and strode from the room.

"Wait! Cass! I can explain."

Spinning to face him, she said, "Explain this. Did you come to Austin to talk us into selling Chili Witches?"

He opened and closed his mouth.

"Cat got your tongue?" she asked in a syrupy voice. "You're lower than worm dirt." She wheeled and headed for the front door, grabbing her purse on the way.

"Cass, please listen to me. It may have started out that way, but I swear to God, things changed. I love—"

She slammed the front door in his face and ran for the elevator.

He yanked open the door and came after her. "Dammit, Cass, you've got to listen."

Poking the elevator button repeatedly, she said, "Go away. My mother was right. She said you were a charlatan! To think that I—we— Oh, gawd! I'm such a gullible fool." She poked the button again, and the door opened.

She rushed inside. Griff followed.

"You can't come in here," she said. "You're naked!"

"I don't care." He wrapped the towel he held around his waist. "Sweetheart, please listen to me. I told Walt the deal was off, and—"

"I'm not listening to you, dirtbag!" She crammed her feet into her shoes. "I should have listened to my first instincts. I knew I couldn't trust you as far as I could throw you. When will I *ever* learn?" She looped her bag over her head and shoulder.

The elevator door opened, and she ran for the sidewalk to elude him, and jogged toward home.

Undeterred, he jogged alongside her, barefoot and bare-assed in downtown Austin, trying to get her to listen to his lousy excuses. She ran faster. "Dammit, Griff, you're naked!"

"I don't care. I love you, Cass. I want to marry you and live in Austin and have babies!"

Oh, gawd. What if she was pregnant?

She ran faster.

At an intersection, a police car pulled alongside them and blocked the way. The cop got out. "Sir. Stop right there."

The light turned and Cass shot across the street. She glanced over her shoulder to see Griff being put into the backseat of the patrol car. Her heart did a little flip, but she steeled herself. "Good enough, you slick weasel," she muttered.

In a few minutes she was home, and as she was about to

go upstairs, Sunny drove up. Cass waited for her to get out of her car.

"Cass, what's wrong?"

"Griffin Mitchell is what's wrong. Mom was right. You were right. Everybody was right. He's a conniving son of a bitch! Did you know he's a partner in ZASM?"

"What's ZASM?"

"Walter Zeagler's ZASM, the company trying to buy us out. Zeagler's the Z, and Griff is probably the M. Griff came here to get in our good graces and cajole us into selling this property."

"How did you find out?"

Cass told Sunny about the phone call and confrontation.

"Oh, dear Lord, Cass. How terrible. I'm so sorry." She hugged her. "What can I do?"

"Nothing, sis. No, you can keep him away from me. I'm going to lock myself upstairs in my apartment. If I know him, he'll be banging on the door any minute trying to 'explain'—as if he could. I'm not answering the phone or my door, and if he tries to wheedle you into anything, don't fall for it. Send him packing."

"You got it. I'll come up later and use our code to knock."

They hugged again, and Cass ran upstairs, noticing only then that her shirt was on backward.

LUCKILY, AUSTIN COPS WERE understanding. The one who'd picked up Griff listened with a fairly straight face to his explanation of his attire. Then took him home.

Luckily as well, the valet in the garage vouched for him. Unfortunately, when Griff got upstairs he discovered he was locked out of his apartment. After a few choice words, he kicked the door, which didn't bother the door but mangled his toe and hurt like hell.

Another trip down the elevator and he located someone with a pass key to let him in. Nobody he met on either trip commented on his dress. Maybe they thought he was wearing a bathing suit under the towel.

First thing he did was call Walt and ask him what the hell he wanted. No, he wouldn't meet with him in Austin next week, and no, he wouldn't change his mind about anything. He quizzed Walt about what he'd said to Cass, yelled a few colorful things about his parentage and brain size, and hung up. He'd begun to think months ago that Walt was losing it. No telling what the crazy bastard would do next. Griff had tried to tell the other partners, but as long as they were making huge profits, they didn't much care.

He'd tried to reason with Walt, showed him research on a dozen other properties, but it was like trying to reason with a gorilla, so Griff had tied up a few loose ends, packed up his office and told them where to stick it.

Somehow, some way, he had to get Cass to listen to him. He wanted to beat his head against a wall. He got dressed and headed for her apartment.

Her car was in its usual place, so he figured she hadn't gone far. He went upstairs and banged on her door for ten minutes, but she didn't answer. He put his ear to the door and could hear the faint noise of her television, so he assumed she was there. Next he tried dialing her cell and was able to make out a ring inside. But she didn't answer. It kicked into voice mail.

He sat down on the steps and tried his best to explain things. He told her he'd resigned from the firm, and poured his heart out to her. Over and over he begged her to forgive him and talk to him.

After knocking one more time, he stuck his phone in his

pocket and went downstairs to Chili Witches. Maybe Sunny could help.

Wrong.

With her hands on her hips, Cass's twin glared at him. "You are reprehensible, Griff Mitchell. You've broken her heart, and what you've done to my sister, you've done to me. You're not welcome in Chili Witches ever again, and I have friends to enforce that request." She nodded toward a table of cops. "*Leave.*"

Griff walked out of Chili Witches, but he couldn't go yet. He went back upstairs and knocked softly on Cass's door. "Cass, please talk to me. Just give me five minutes. Please."

Nothing.

He sat down on the steps and tried to think of a way to get to her, short of battering the door down—which would only set off the alarm and cause havoc.

Griff called a florist and offer them a bonus if they would deliver a huge arrangement ASAP.

In twenty minutes, a florist van stopped and a kid got out carrying a big vase of mixed flowers, pretty ones. The kid nodded to Griff as he passed him sitting on the stairs. The delivery boy knocked and waited. Knocked and waited. Nothing.

"Mister," the kid said. "Do you know the lady who lives here?"

Griff nodded.

"Would you give these to her, please?"

"Just leave them by the door," Griff said.

"I don't know…" the kid looked at the sky. "It might rain."

"Leave them."

He shrugged, set them by the door and hurried down the stairs to his van. Griff watched and waited. The door didn't open, and the flowers seemed to mock him.

For the next five hours, two of them in the rain, he sat on

the stairs, alternately phoning and knocking until his battery ran out of juice and his shoes were full of water. Temporarily conceding defeat, he sloshed to his car and went home.

He gave the Marcia Ball tickets to the valet, went upstairs and took a hot shower, and tried to think of a better strategy.

THE ENTIRE TIME GRIFF pounded on her door, Cass had been sitting on her couch eating Cheerios from a box and watching old movies. And crying. Initially, her anger had fueled her, but in the end, grief overtook her and drained her dry.

She'd heard him go, listened as he plodded down the stairs in the rain, watched out the window as his car left the lot. Only when she was sure he'd gone did she open the door and peek out. The poor flowers were getting pounded by the rain. She took them in and set them in the kitchen sink to perk back up.

The bouquet might recover, but she wondered if she ever would.

Chapter Twenty-Four

Cass didn't sleep much, and she dreamed awful things she couldn't remember, but kept waking her up when she dozed off. She finally got up, took a couple of aspirin and put cold compresses on her swollen eyes. Nothing had ever hurt her so deeply as this. Daniel's betrayal was nothing compared to Griff's.

Mostly, she realized, because she hadn't loved Daniel so much.

Well, she refused to waste any more tears over Griff and his devious ways. She was determined to gut up and go on. Today was a workday for her.

Her phone rang. He was starting early. She removed the compress to look at the caller ID. Sunny.

"Good morning, sis," Cass said in her cheeriest voice. "How are you today?"

"The question is, Cass, how are you?"

"I'm fine. Just fine."

"You don't sound fine. You're croaking like a frog."

"Must have been all the yelling I did yesterday."

"Yeah, sure," Sunny said. "I know you must feel like crap. How about I work for you today?"

"No. Absolutely not. You're not going to cancel your plans.

Mom and Aunt Min have been excited out of their minds about meeting with your wedding planner and getting started on the details today."

"They're excited. I'm not. This is my second marriage. Ben and I want a simple ceremony in the backyard and a lemon cake from the bakery down the street."

"I know. Keep reminding them."

"Have you heard any more from Griff?"

"Not a peep. I think he finally got the message."

"I hope so. If he gives you any trouble, call me and I'll send somebody to toss him out."

Cass laughed for the first time in nearly twenty-four hours. "You forget I have a baseball bat under my bed."

"Seriously, Cass, call me if you need me. Should I tell Mom and Aunt Min about this?"

"No. I feel like enough of a fool without everybody knowing about it. Just play dumb, and later I'll tell them things didn't work out for us. Mom will be thrilled."

After she hung up, Cass wandered into the bathroom and stared at her reflection. Talk about being "rode hard and put away wet." She looked worse than terrible, but her eyes didn't seem quite so puffy after the compress, and her headache had eased some. After showering and dressing, she took half an hour to skillfully apply a ton of makeup without it looking troweled on. Not bad.

She pasted a grin on her face. "It's showtime."

Downstairs, she unlocked the back door for arriving employees and began her usual routine. Her phone rang and she jumped three feet. Pulling her cell from her pocket, she saw the POAC secretary's name and answered. After they ended the call, Cass checked her voice mail and noted twenty-seven messages from Griff. She should have deleted them immediately, but some masochistic perversion had kept her from it. She might even listen to them someday when she needed reminding what an idiot she'd been.

Lunchtime came and went without incident. They had a moderate crowd. With the nearby government offices closed, Saturdays usually weren't extremely busy.

About three-thirty, Griff walked in the front door. He hadn't shaved, his blue eyes were bloodshot and he generally looked like hell.

She met him before he got too far inside. "Griff, please leave. We have nothing more to say."

"Will you give me at least five minutes, Cass? I need to talk to you."

"Not today."

"When? If I call you tomorrow or come by, will you talk to me?" His eyes seemed to plead, and she almost caved.

"I don't know. There is one question I'd like to ask you, and I'd like a truthful answer."

"Anything," he said. "Ask it."

"Was ZASM responsible for the break-in and flooding here?"

"I swear to God, Cass, I knew nothing about it and was in no way responsible." He closed his eyes for a moment, then opened them. He had the most woebegone expression she'd ever seen as he looked her straight in the eye and sucked in a deep breath. "However, I've had my suspicions about Walt. I can't be sure, but he might have done it. The man is crazy."

Cass thought she might faint, and her voice quavered as she said, "And this man is your partner? What the hell kind of business are you involved in? Where are your ethics? I've heard enough. Please leave. Now."

"Cass—"

"I don't want to hear another word. If you don't leave

quietly, I'll have you thrown out, and if you persist in bothering me, I'll get a restraining order." She turned and walked away before she had a total meltdown.

Hiding out in the office, she sat behind the desk and buried her face in her hands. What was wrong with her? As she'd stood talking to Griff, a terrible longing had come over her, and she'd wanted to throw herself into his arms and have him hold her and comfort her. Was she stark raving mad? He was the cause of her pain.

She clenched her teeth and laced her fingers tightly together until her shaking stopped. She would get through this, she told herself over and over like a mantra. She was a survivor.

BUSINESS PICKED UP FOR dinner, and she was pleased to see several old friends. Ben McKee's sister and brother-in-law, Tracy and Rick, stopped in with their two little girls.

"We've come for the bestest chili in the world," the younger one said.

"And some larrupin' peach cobbler," the other one added. "Uncle Ben says larrupin' means delicious."

Cass smiled, really smiled, showed them to a table and chatted for a short while. A few minutes later, she was surprised to see Greg Gonzales come in with two women, one older, one younger.

She hurried to the door to meet them. "Hi, Greg. Good to see you."

He introduced his mother and younger sister, Donna, who appeared to have Down syndrome. Cass greeted them warmly and seated them near the window. "Greg, life has been pretty hectic for me, but I plan to spend tomorrow afternoon making the rest of my selections, and I'll have my choices ready for you by Monday."

"Sounds good. I've been telling Donna and my mother about the chili here, and Mama's been itching to come and steal your recipe."

"Oh, Greg!" his mother said, chuckling.

"I don't like chili," Donna said, screwing up her face. "But I like hamburgers."

"I'm glad to hear that, Donna," Cass said. "Our hamburgers are really, really good. Some say the best in Texas."

Donna beamed.

"Let me take your drink orders, and I'll send over a waiter right away."

Martin Sevier from the POAC board brought his family for dinner, as did Sunny's former partner in Homicide. It seemed to be old home night with the number of friends and regulars who showed up.

Cass stood with her hand on the bar and smiled as she looked out over the diners, listened to the buzz of conversation punctuated by laughter. The smells of chili and onions and sizzling meat were as familiar to her as her own reflection, as were the kitschy decorations on the walls. These sights and sounds and smells were woven into the fabric of her life, and they comforted her. She rubbed her fingers over the bar's smooth wood, where so many fingers had touched before.

Dear God, she loved this place.

CASS FELT CONSIDERABLY BETTER when she said goodbye to the last of the staff and made her final walk through Chili Witches. She glanced toward a corner, catching a movement there, and froze when she saw the Senator sitting at the table, a coffee cup in front of him. No matter how many times she encountered him, she would never get used to seeing a ghost.

"Good evening, Senator. What brings you here?"

"Do I need a reason to drop in?" He looked a bit sad.

"Things are off between Griff and me."

He nodded. "I'm sorry to hear that. I like him."

"Mom doesn't. She'll be delighted."

"He truly loves you, you know. If I had to guess, I'd say Griffin is your soul mate, your destiny. You've been very good for each other. Listen to your heart, Cass."

"But he lied and came here to use me for his own ends."

"Did he? Are you sure?"

The Senator was gone.

And she was confused.

Suddenly weary to the bone, she set the security alarm, locked up and went upstairs. She gathered all her house samples together and put them in her tote bag by her laptop. After she undressed and pulled on her boxers and a tank top, Cass fixed herself a bowl of strawberry ice cream with chocolate sauce and pecans, and curled up in bed to eat it.

What exactly was the Senator trying to say to her? *Soul mates? Destiny?* Sounded like so much hokum. Griff was a warty toad. Sure, he had her going for a while, and he was hell on wheels in bed, but great sex wasn't all it was cracked up to be. It couldn't replace respect.

She yawned. Setting her bowl aside, she turned out the light and pulled the covers over her head.

SOMETIME DURING THE night Cass was jolted awake by a pounding on her door. "Dammit, Griff!" she yelled. "Go away!" She covered her head with a pillow to drown out the noise, and slapped at her alarm clock, which was going like crazy.

Her phone began to ring, joining the other raucous ringing and clanging and beeping going on.

What was that smell?

She jolted upright and grabbed her phone. Hank Wisda.

When she answered, he yelled, "Get out, Cass! Get out! Hurry! The place is on fire!"

She began to cough as smoke seeped into the room.

Chapter Twenty-Five

Cass ran for the exit, grabbing whatever she could on her way. The smoke grew thicker, and she heard Hank still pounding on her door. Yanking it open, she fell outside. Flames shot up behind her.

Hank yelled, "Quick! Get as far away as you can!"

"Call 9-1-1!"

"Trucks are on their way. Go! Go!"

She ran out to the parking lot. Thankfully, her purse was one of the things she'd grabbed, and she fished out her keys as she ran. Quickly unlocking her car, she tossed her armload of stuff inside, drove two blocks away and parked. Fire trucks and police cars screamed by her, and as she looked back over her shoulder, fire had completely engulfed the lower floor and flames were shooting up fifty feet or more over the roof. She could hear the whoosh and crackle from where she sat, watching as a window of her apartment blew out.

She had her cell phone as well, and she immediately dialed Sunny. Weeping hysterically now, Cass said, "Come quick. Chili Witches is on fire! Hank and I are okay."

Holding her steering wheel in a death grip, Cass fought to

calm herself. What else? What else bad could happen? Her nerves were stretched to breaking.

More police cars and fire trucks screamed by, and great streams of water poured over the fire, but the inferno raged on. Cass pawed through the items she'd been able to save, hoping for clothes to put on. The closest thing she found was the blue chenille throw from the couch. She'd saved her laptop, her tote of color samples, a painting her mom had done that had hung near the door, and one left shoe. A red high heeled sandal.

The sum total of her belongings was what she had in her car. The little stuffed cat, all her clothes, the box of medals and memorabilia from high school and college, her furniture, her jewelry—everything was gone. Everything.

But she was alive. Hank was alive. Stuff could be replaced.

But Chili Witches… She choked on a sob.

Cass got out of her car and locked it, carrying with her only her phone, her keys and the chenille throw, and walked back toward the conflagration, where flames and glowing embers licked the sky and drank the gushing streams of water.

SUNNY PASSED HER ON the way and screeched to a stop at the curb. Jumping from her car, she ran to her sister. "Oh my God, Cass. Oh my God."

They hugged each other and sobbed.

"What happened?" Sunny asked.

"I don't know. The downstairs was already burning and my apartment was getting smoky when Hank managed to wake me. Did you call Mom and Aunt Min?"

"Yes. I told them not to come, but they're already on their way." She looked down at Cass's feet. "Where are your shoes?"

Cass shrugged.

"Wait a minute. I think I have something in the trunk." Sunny ran to her car and popped the back. She returned in a minute with her gardening boots. "This is the best I can do."

"Sold," Cass said. She brushed off her feet and stuck them into the boots. Pulling the chenille throw around her shoulders, she trudged with her twin toward the fire.

Police had blocked off the area, so they couldn't get too close, but they saw their mother and aunt, disheveled and distraught, running toward them.

"Are you okay?" Gloria asked. "What happened?"

Cass shrugged. "I don't know. It obviously started somewhere downstairs—either at Hooks or Chili Witches."

Holding each other, the four of them watched the building burn.

"My stars and garters," Gloria moaned, shoving her fist against her mouth. "I can't believe it."

Tears trickled down Aunt Min's face. "Oh my, at the memories burning with that place! It's gone, isn't it?"

Sunny nodded. "No way to save anything. They can only keep it from spreading to surrounding buildings."

GRIFF COULDN'T SLEEP. He hadn't been able to since Cass left. He stood at the window, staring at a spot to the west of the capitol grounds where he knew Chili Witches stood. Because of buildings in the way, he couldn't see the actual structure or Cass's apartment, but he knew exactly where it was.

He frowned. A bright glow lit the sky where he looked. Was that a fire? His pulse kicked into overdrive. Could it be Chili Witches? Cass!

He had to find out if she was okay. It was three o'clock in the morning, and there wasn't a chance in hell she would answer if he called.

In record time he laced on his running shoes, stuck his keys and wallet in his pocket and hurried downstairs. As soon as he hit the street he could hear the sirens and smell the fire.

Panicked, he ran toward the activity, his long strides eating up the pavement. The closer he got, the more his panic grew. Oh, hell! It *was* Chili Witches! He prayed and ran faster.

The area was blocked off and hoses poured water onto the roaring, raging flames. He tried to get through but was stopped at every turn.

"Cass!" he yelled, running around the perimeter of the barricade. "Cass!" Terror clawed at his insides. "Cass!"

At last he saw four women standing beside a sawhorse. One wore rubber boots and a blanket.

"Cass!"

She turned.

He ran toward her, grabbed her and held her tight. He held her and swung her around and kissed her face all over. "I've never been so scared in all my life."

She struggled in his arms. "Let me go! Dammit! Let me go."

He set her down, but held her at arm's length and scanned her from head to toe. "Thank God you're okay. You are, aren't you?"

"I'm okay, but Chili Witches isn't. It's gone. Nothing but ashes will be left. Are you happy now?"

Griff felt the blood drain from his face. "You can't believe I had anything to do with this! Cass, I swear by all that's holy, I would never do anything to hurt or endanger you. You have to believe me."

"Go away, Griff. Just go away. I want to be with my family now."

He didn't want to go. He wanted to hold her in his arms and wash the soot from her face. But in the end he left. She was safe. That's what was important now.

By early morning, Chili Witches and Hooks were blackened skeletons of one-hundred-and-twenty-year-old jagged, broken bones and heaps of smoldering ashes. Sid and Foster stood beside their little group, looking dazed and lost. Ben, who'd heard about the fire on the early news, had his arm wrapped around Sunny. Cass stood between her mom and aunt, squeezing their hands.

"I suppose it's over," Gloria said. "There's nothing we can do here. Let's go home and get some rest."

"I agree," Min said. "I'm exhausted. Did all our insurance papers burn?"

"No," Sunny said. "I have them in a lockbox at my house. Cass, come home with me. I have an extra bedroom and clothes you can wear."

Cass nodded, then turned to the owners of Hooks. She hugged Sid and Foster. "Guys, I'm so sorry about this. What can we do to help?"

"There's nothing you can do," Sid said.

"We're fully covered by insurance," Foster added, "so we can take our time about deciding our next step."

"Does someone need to stay and talk to the authorities?" Cass asked.

"I'll handle things," Ben said. "All of you go on home. You look like you're about to drop."

Slowly they hugged and dispersed. Cass followed Sunny home and took her meager pile of belongings inside with her.

Cass stood in the shower for the longest time, soaping off the soot and washing the smell from her hair. The water seemed to help. By the time she was finished, Sunny had left a nightshirt and clothes for her. There was no point in trying to sleep, Cass was too agitated. She felt like crap, and to top things off, she'd started her period. Thank God. To have been pregnant would have been the last straw.

Opting for yoga pants and a tee, she dressed and padded into the kitchen in search of coffee.

"Coffee's dripping," Sunny said. "I didn't figure you could sleep."

"Not on your life. My brain's like a hornet's nest. Have you ever felt like a black cloud was hovering over you and following you wherever you went?"

"Oh, yeah." Sunny poured two mugs and added sugar and cream.

They took their coffee into the living room and curled up on the couch.

"Think Mom and Aunt Min will want to rebuild?" Cass asked.

"I don't know. Things wouldn't be the same."

"Nope. Sunny, this breaks my heart. A part of history burned this morning. The town's history, our family's history. I already feel like a big chunk of me is missing."

Sunny only nodded. They felt the same way. "You don't think Griff had anything to do with the fire, do you?"

"Not really. No. I can't imagine he would sanction such a thing. If Hank hadn't awakened me, I could be dead. The security alarm and the smoke alarm were going off like crazy, and the noise didn't faze me."

Sunny shuddered. "I don't like to think about it."

"Me either." She took another swallow of coffee. "Thankfully, I saved my purse, along with my checkbook and credit cards. I need everything from the skin out. I don't own a hair drier or a toothbrush or shoes. Nothing. I can't even recharge my phone."

"Don't you have a charger in your car?"

"I do, now that you've reminded me, but I don't want to have to ride around to juice up my battery. I need to make a list of essentials. Help me. It'll keep our mind off…everything."

When the list grew to three pages, Cass stopped and they prioritized. Personal grooming items, makeup, a simple basic wardrobe, charger for her phone.

"Want to go with me?" Cass asked.

"Sure."

Their first stop was Ulta. The second was IHOP. The third was Nordstrom's. By the time they got to Best Buy, their tail feathers were dragging.

"Tell me this is all for today," Sunny said.

"This is all. I promise. Let's go home and order a pizza. I'm starved."

When they arrived at Sunny's they found two food bags from Cass's favorite Italian restaurant sitting by the back door.

Griff. Cass knew immediately this was from him. Before she could stop herself, a warm feeling stole over her and she smiled. No, dammit. She wouldn't be suckered in by shrimp Portofino. She sighed. But she wouldn't let the pasta go to waste, either.

Ben stopped by to bring them up to date, and he shared their meal.

"From the preliminary investigation by the fire department," he said, "it looks like the fire started in the office at Chili Witches."

"But how?" Sunny asked.

"Not sure," Ben said, "but the safe survived and it looks like somebody had been after it with a cutting torch."

"You mean a *thief* started the fire?" Cass asked.

"Maybe. Or the damage to the safe may have been caused during the fire. As I say, this is preliminary information. We'll know more in a few days."

"The alarm was set," Cass said. "I distinctly remember setting it. How could someone have gotten past it?"

Ben shrugged. "An investigator will be out to talk with you tomorrow."

"I'm going to leave it with you two," Cass said. "I'm going to put up all my stuff and sack out." On her way to the guest room, she paused at the bookshelf to select a novel and tucked it under her arm.

After she'd hung up her new and much abbreviated wardrobe and stowed her shoes—one pair of pewter flats, one pair of sport shoes, one pair of beige thongs and one pair of black heels—she brushed her teeth with her new brush and changed into her new nightie. Socks and undies went in a dresser drawer. She hooked up her phone to the new charger and climbed in bed with Janet Evanovich. She'd only made it to page three when her phone rang. Maddie.

"Hey, Maddie, what's up?"

"Cass, I have the poop on Griff Mitchell. My brother knows him, but not well. My cousin Will is a friend of his. They still play racquetball or one of those guy games. Griff was a supersmart stud at Harvard Law, and he worked for a firm in New York for a while. About five years ago he and three other buddies from undergrad days formed a consulting company. ZASM. Walter Zeagler, Peter Adair, Fisher Smith and Griffin Mitchell. They partner with developers of hotels and high-rises in a variety of capacities, particularly acquiring properties, and they've made scads of money doing it.

"Will said Griff had been in Texas scouting properties, but he came back into town a week or so ago madder than hell at one of the partners, and quit the firm. Packed up his desk and told them he didn't like the way they did business and to go to hell. Will was stunned. We're talking about thumbing his nose at megabucks."

Cass sat straight up in bed. "He did?"

"According to my cousin, he did. And Will also got the idea he'd fallen in love with a woman in Texas because he was selling everything, and told Will not to expect him back. That woman wouldn't happen to be you, would it?"

"How did you come to that conclusion?"

Maddie laughed. "I didn't get where I am on my looks. Are you the one?"

"There are some problems."

"I'd try to work them out if I were you. This Griff sounds like a keeper. Will's very fond of him, and Will is quite discerning. Does my information help?"

"Perhaps. I'll need some time to process what you've told me. Is there any way I can return the favor?"

"Sure," Maddie said. "Invite me to the wedding."

"Don't pack your bags just yet."

They chatted for a few minutes about mutual acquaintances, but Cass didn't mention the fire or anything more about Griff.

After they said goodbye, she lay back and stared at the ceiling. Had she judged Griff too quickly and too harshly?

Maybe she had.

She picked up her phone again and listened to her messages from Griff—all twenty-seven of them.

By the time she'd heard him pour his heart out, she was in tears. She knew without a doubt that he loved her, and everything he'd told her was true.

She got up, dressed and packed a few items in a Nordstrom's bag. Sunny's bedroom door was closed, so Cass left her a note on the kitchen counter and tiptoed out.

She drove to Griff's high-rise, went upstairs and knocked.

When he opened the door, she knew he was surprised to see her.

"Griff, let's talk."

THEY TALKED FOR A LONG, long time. A small voice inside her whispered that his words were true. She loved him. She trusted him. She could only follow her heart. One chapter of her life had closed; this was a new beginning.

When Griff held her and kissed her and made her spirit sing, she understood what the Senator had meant. She felt as if she'd found her soul mate and come home.

Epilogue

The evening was already in full swing when Cass and Griff arrived. Griff would have rented a ballroom at the hotel if she had agreed. She'd insisted on a less ostentatious room and a small band for dancing.

And people were dancing. The entire Outlaw bunch had turned out, and Sam was twirling Gloria around the floor, while J.J. partnered Min. What a difference a year made, Cass thought as they made their way through the crowd.

Mom and Aunt Min had decided not to rebuild Chili Witches. They'd been very philosophical about the fire and the loss of their business. Perhaps it was God's way of ending that phase of their lives. They'd insisted the twins should follow their own dreams, not tie themselves to the café as they had. Sunny had seemed relieved by the decision, and to tell the truth, Cass was, too. They'd sold the property—not to ZASM, but to someone else.

Maybe the thieves had done them a favor. Using tapes from a surveillance camera on a nearby building, the police had caught the culprits a week after Chili Witches was destroyed. The pair, a busboy and a floor installer, had entered through Hooks, using the alarm code the busboy had stolen from his bosses. They'd sawed a hole between the men's room in Hooks and the office in Chili Witches, determined to crack the big safe the floor installer had seen there. They'd only succeeded in setting the office afire before they fled. The camera had caught them both full face, as well as their getaway car.

Cass greeted several members of POAC as they neared the podium, as well as old friends from high school and college, and new friends she'd met more recently. Sunny was there with Ben, of course, her tummy just beginning to show a little pooch.

Griff, grinning like a possum, stepped up to the microphone. "Ladies and gentlemen, may I have your attention, please." The band played an ending, and the crowd turned to the raised stage. "For those of you who don't know me, I'm Griffin Mitchell, campaign manager for our esteemed candidate. The polls have closed. The votes have been counted, and our new city councilwoman—elected without a runoff—is Cassidy Outlaw Mitchell!"

The band struck up a lively song and everybody applauded wildly as balloons—again, Griff's idea—fell from the ceiling. Griff whirled her around the dance floor, and Cass laughed from the pure joy of the moment and the love of her husband, family and friends. Her mother and Aunt Min had eventually fallen in love with Griff, especially after he took over the franchising of Chili Witches and made them loads of money.

Cass danced with every Outlaw there, including Wes. She even made a round of the floor with Ben, who was an excellent dancer, and Greg Gonzales, who was no slouch, either.

As they toasted with champagne, Griff held her close to his side. "Have I told you lately that I love you?"

She grinned up at him. "Not in the past half hour or so."

"Well, I do. The day you tripped over me on the jogging trail was the luckiest day of my life. I love you, Cass. Heart and soul."

* * * * *

Harlequin offers a romance for every mood!
See below for a sneak peek from
our suspense romance line
Silhouette® Romantic Suspense.
Introducing HER HERO IN HIDING by
New York Times *bestselling author Rachel Lee.*

Kay Young returned to woozy consciousness to find that she was lying on a soft sofa beneath a heap of quilts near a cheerfully burning fire. When she tried to move, however, everything hurt, and she groaned.

At once she heard a sound, then a stranger with a hard, harsh face was squatting beside her. "Shh," he said softly. "You're safe here. I promise."

"I have to go," she said weakly, struggling against pain. "He'll find me. He can't find me."

"Easy, lady," he said quietly. "You're hurt. No one's going to find you here."

"He will," she said desperately, terror clutching at her insides. "He always finds me!"

"Easy," he said again. "There's a blizzard outside. No one's getting here tonight, not even the doctor. I know, because I tried."

"Doctor? I don't need a doctor! I've got to get away."

"There's nowhere to go tonight," he said levelly. "And if I thought you could stand, I'd take you to a window and show you."

But even as she tried once more to pull away the quilts, she remembered something else: this man had been gentle when he'd found her beside the road, even when she had kicked and clawed. He hadn't hurt her.

Terror receded just a bit. She looked at him and detected signs of true concern there.

The terror eased another notch and she let her head sag on the pillow. "He always finds me," she whispered.

"Not here. Not tonight. That much I can guarantee."

Will Kay's mysterious rescuer
protect her from her worst fears?
Find out in HER HERO IN HIDING
by New York Times bestselling author Rachel Lee.
Available June 2010, only from
Silhouette® Romantic Suspense.

HARLEQUIN® *Romance*®

GIRLS' Weekend in VEGAS

Four friends, four dream weddings!

On a girly weekend in Las Vegas, best friends Alex, Molly,
Serena and Jayne are supposed to just have fun and forget
men, but they end up meeting their perfect matches!
Will the love they find in Vegas stay in Vegas?

Find out in this sassy, fun and wildly romantic miniseries
all about love and friendship!

═══════════════════

Saving Cinderella! by MYRNA MACKENZIE
Available June

Vegas Pregnancy Surprise by SHIRLEY JUMP
Available July

Inconveniently Wed! by JACKIE BRAUN
Available August

Wedding Date with the Best Man
by MELISSA MCCLONE
Available September

Desire

From *USA TODAY* bestselling author

LEANNE BANKS

CEO'S EXPECTANT SECRETARY

Elle Linton is hiding more than just her affair
with her boss Brock Maddox. And she's
terrifed that if their secret turns public her
mother's life may be put at risk. When she
unexpectedly becomes pregnant she's forced
to make a decision. Will she be able to save
her relationship and her mother's life?

*Available June
wherever books are sold.*

Always Powerful, Passionate and Provocative.

REQUEST YOUR FREE BOOKS!
2 FREE NOVELS PLUS 2 FREE GIFTS!

HARLEQUIN®

American Romance®

Love, Home & Happiness!

YES! Please send me 2 FREE Harlequin® American Romance® novels and my 2 FREE gifts (gifts are worth about $10). After receiving them, if I don't wish to receive any more books, I can return the shipping statement marked "cancel." If I don't cancel, I will receive 4 brand-new novels every month and be billed just $4.24 per book in the U.S. or $4.99 per book in Canada. That's a saving of at least 15% off the cover price! It's quite a bargain! Shipping and handling is just 50¢ per book.* I understand that accepting the 2 free books and gifts places me under no obligation to buy anything. I can always return a shipment and cancel at any time. Even if I never buy another book from Harlequin, the two free books and gifts are mine to keep forever.

154/354 HDN E5LG

Name _____ (PLEASE PRINT)

Address _____ Apt. #

City _____ State/Prov. _____ Zip/Postal Code

Signature (if under 18, a parent or guardian must sign)

Mail to the Harlequin Reader Service:
IN U.S.A.: P.O. Box 1867, Buffalo, NY 14240-1867
IN CANADA: P.O. Box 609, Fort Erie, Ontario L2A 5X3

Not valid for current subscribers to Harlequin® American Romance® books.

Want to try two free books from another line?
Call 1-800-873-8635 or visit www.morefreebooks.com.

* Terms and prices subject to change without notice. Prices do not include applicable taxes. N.Y. residents add applicable sales tax. Canadian residents will be charged applicable provincial taxes and GST. Offer not valid in Quebec. This offer is limited to one order per household. All orders subject to approval. Credit or debit balances in a customer's account(s) may be offset by any other outstanding balance owed by or to the customer. Please allow 4 to 6 weeks for delivery. Offer available while quantities last.

Your Privacy: Harlequin is committed to protecting your privacy. Our Privacy Policy is available online at www.eHarlequin.com or upon request from the Reader Service. From time to time we make our lists of customers available to reputable third parties who have a product or service of interest to you. If you would prefer we not share your name and address, please check here. ☐

Help us get it right—We strive for accurate, respectful and relevant communications. To clarify or modify your communication preferences, visit us at www.ReaderService.com/consumerschoice.

HAR10R

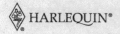
HARLEQUIN®

Showcase

On sale May 11, 2010

Reader favorites from the most talented voices in romance

Save $1.00 on the purchase of 1 or more Harlequin® Showcase books.

SAVE $1.00 on the purchase of 1 or more Harlequin® Showcase books.

Coupon expires Oct 31, 2010. Redeemable at participating retail outlets.
Limit one coupon per purchase. Valid in the U.S.A. and Canada only.

52609015

5 65373 00076 2   (8100)0 11651

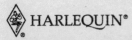
HARLEQUIN®

American ★ Romance®

COMING NEXT MONTH

Available June 8, 2010

#1309 THE SHERIFF AND THE BABY
Babies & Bachelors USA
C.C. Coburn

#1310 WALKER: THE RODEO LEGEND
The Codys: The First Family of Rodeo
Rebecca Winters

#1311 THE BEST MAN IN TEXAS
Tanya Michaels

#1312 SECOND CHANCE HERO
Shelley Galloway

www.eHarlequin.com

HARCNMBPA0510